Having grown up in the 60s watching Star Trek and the lunar landings, space and its exploration has always been of great interest. With Mars now the next target for mankind and more and more information becoming available about this mysterious planet, it seemed the perfect time for this story to be told.

David T Bennett

SMAR

AUSTIN MACAULEY PUBLISHERS™

LONDON • CAMBRIDGE • NEW YORK • SHARJAH

A CIP catalogue record for this title is available from the British Library.

ISBN 9781398422575 (Paperback)
ISBN 9781398422582 (ePub e-book)

www.austinmacauley.com

First Published (2021)
Austin Macauley Publishers Ltd
25 Canada Square
Canary Wharf
London
E14 5LQ

Chapter 1

Topside

Tega sat beside the fire warming himself in the cold Smarian night air. The purple haze of the night sky that engulfed everything being held back only by the glow of the fire light. He watched as each flame danced in celebration of its brief life before disappearing forever into the abyss of the night sky. Tega pulled his blanket tighter around himself and grunted. He didn't see the beauty in the flames nor basked in the wonder as it made the shadows join in its dance. He was only interested in the warmth that it gave him on yet another bitter night. One of far too many that he had endured in the many years he had spent on Topside.

For him there was no beauty on the Smarian Topside landscape. All he saw was a very inhospitable place where nothing grew amidst the rocks and the red dust that covered the planet and certainly no one with any sense lived there. The huge barren deserts stretched for as far as the eye could see with their hidden lakes of quicksand awaiting anyone who was unfortunate enough to find themselves out there. One step and the ground would swallow you up. No one would hear you scream as slowly you were sucked down into the sand to disappear into and become part of that desolate landscape.

The harder you struggled, the quicker the sand would gulp you up. Resistance was futile. The winds would whisk up the sand into a swirling sea sending waves of sand crashing around all the rocks and crevices until it destroyed any footsteps or tracks in its path. Removing any sign of you and any sign of you ever being there. Returning the landscape back to a red dead rock. The deserts were broken up only by the vast rugged mountain ranges that reached up and almost touched the bright red sky. From their base at the edge of the desert to the very top, they were immense. Like pathways to the stars, with the occasional cave offering you sanctuary from the constant and bitter winds and sandstorms that ravaged the Smarian landscape. But beware, once you ventured into their wide ravines that ran for miles and miles looking for refuge, they had you. Their steep sides began to close in until they became narrow passes that seemed to call to you to go further. Further into the maze of pathways that twisted and turned on their never-ending way to nowhere. At each turn a glimmer of hope that safety was around the corner only to be dashed by yet another spiteful multiple choice of directions. The only choice being to make a choice without knowing what the outcome or consequence that each one would bring. Travelling so far in that going back was no longer an option as you could never, never find the path whence you came.

Travelling on Topside was indeed a treacherous affair. That along with the constant bitter cold would make it a place that you didn't really want to visit unless you really, really had to. Only the scouts survived out there with their meagre supplies and one-man-tents to keep them safe from the cold and wind. Sometimes it was so bad that they would have to stay in one spot for days at a time until the storms let up. To venture outside the safe haven of their tents was suicide when the storms raged. But Tega didn't mind. He had spent most of his life out there on Topside.

Originally he was sent there as a punishment for speaking out against the 'Great One' as was the crime that most of the Smarians were sent there for. But he was lucky. He had been taught how to survive by one of the best scouts ever, Hundrey. Tega had never seen Topside before he was sent there. Indeed all he had ever known of it was from a few pictures and the rumours of its enormous wastelands where Smarians such as he would get lost and go mad wandering around until they died. Being sent to Topside for a year's punishment was generally a death sentence for most. Only the hardiest and most determined ever survived to tell the tale and then, as they never wanted to go there again, they wouldn't commit their 'crime' again. For the Smarian council it worked a treat! Nothing like a harsh existence for a year to get people to conform to the rule of the 'Great One', if indeed they survived at all. Some of the council thought it was a waste of equipment and food and that they should be just deposited on Topside and left to their own devices but the 'Great One' thought that might be too harsh.

"Give them the chance to come to their senses amidst the loneliness of the wastelands," he thought, always aware of public opinion but never really caring much about it.

Tega had survived many years out there, thanks to his teachings from Hundrey. From the first day that Tega was 'made' a scout, he had always followed the advice of Hundrey. Sticking to him like a homeless puppy, Tega had followed Hundrey across the wastelands for many a year.

Tega had listened intently to everything that Hundrey told him about surviving the wastelands. Watching and learning all the time, Tega had got to know all the stories that Hundrey would tell him around the campfires at night. From Hundrey's early days as a scout to the time they built the current base from the ruins of the old Hundrey would continue into the night. The bottles of beer helped Tega's imagination fill in the gaps left in Hundrey's stories due to old age and the many years out on the wastelands.

Although some of the stories that Hundrey had told about ancient civilisations that had lived Topside aeons ago, Tega had thought, were mainly due to Hundrey living on Topside for far too long. A race that lived above ground all year in cities carved out of the rock of the mountains and were technically advanced was total tosh! *After all*, he thought, *there would be some kind of traces of them but he had never found any*. Sure there were hundreds of caves and caverns in the mountains but they were all natural, weren't they? *How to survive* had been the things that Tega had listened to, not all the other rubbish. Tega had done his punishment years ago but had decided to stay on Topside because he hadn't changed his views and didn't want to give the council the satisfaction of sending him back. Now he had become one of the best scouts around. He had survived longer than most and knew the ever-changing landscape well. He never returned to base unless he had to. Only for rations and to let them know that he was still alive, did he return three or four times a year to that place. But this time was different. This time he had seen it fall to Smar from the night sky. Like a shooting star, at first. A ball of fire falling from the heavens but then slowing down as it made its way through the atmosphere. Tega remembered how captivating it had been, watching it get closer and bigger from a tiny spec of light to something that lit up the night sky. It had taken a while for Tega to realise that this was no ordinary shooting star as he was quite used to seeing strange lights that travelled across the sky every night from one side to the other. Always following the same path, night after night. But this one didn't travel across the sky. This one was falling from it right towards Tega! He had got out of his sleeping bag and had packed up his equipment as quickly as he could always keep a close eye on the object falling from the sky. He got out his binoculars and looked directly at the object. It was still slowing down as it fell to Smar. A blaze of fire and light engulfing whatever was in the centre. Flames and sparks shooting out in all directions as the object got closer and closer lighting up the wastelands as if it was daylight. A light show like he had never seen before. At one point what looked like giant wings sprang from its back, billowing out to form three huge domes that were slowing the object down as it made its descent.

As it got closer to the ground, it slowed even further until you could make out a huge silver object with fire breathing from its belly, scorching the red dust black with its ferocity as it slowly but finally hit the ground. Its huge domes dropping slowly and gracefully to the floor all around the object. The fire stopped once it had landed and was still but the object still glowed red with the heat. Tega kept his distance and carried on looking through his binoculars. Nothing! After a while, he decided that he would take a closer look but the heat from the object was still quite intense so he had to back off. Stopping only once to pick something up. Something that had fallen off the object as it landed. It was still red hot and Tega had to use his gloves and an old blanket but managed to retrieve it and put it in his backpack. Tega made his way back to camp constantly turning around, in case something, anything was watching or following him.

Once back at camp, Tega sat by the fire where he took out the piece and studied it. It was cooler now and Tega could make out that it was made from some kind of metallic material. Unlike any rock that had previously fallen from the sky that Tega had seen, this piece was smooth as if it had been manufactured by someone or something. It was covered with symbols unlike anything that Tega had ever seen. Not random symbols but structured in a way as if it meant something. *This was worth returning to base for*, he thought. As it was nearly dawn, Tega packed up his tent and put the fire out. He had marked its landing place on his map and headed back to the base to tell the commandant the news. The news that no one wanted to hear. The news that another one had made its way through and landed again on Smar!

The base was not a pretty place to be. A huge grey domed building, housing everything from parade ground to sleeping dorms, classrooms to canteens. Full of all the basics anyone would need but scarce on home comforts. Strategically placed smack bang in the middle of the desert surrounded by a high reinforced fence to keep out the worst of the wind and sandstorms. The fence was ringed with lookout posts to warn of any oncoming storms so that the whole place could batten down the hatches and sit it out. It also served to keep people from wandering off into the desert by accident or by choice! It was a very harsh existence at the base and it wasn't unaccustomed to people attempting to escape. However, the base being surrounded by desert in all directions meant that escape wasn't really an option. The entrance to Below was miles and miles away and no one could survive the desert without help and rations. If caught trying to escape home, you were immediately considered as someone who thought they could survive out there on Topside so you were made a scout and dumped as far away as possible and banned from returning for months, hopefully returning that is, not that the hierarchy really cared if you didn't! This was where all new 'recruits' were sent for basic training. Recruits! As all Smarians were required by law to do one year's national service, you couldn't really call them 'recruits'. Conscripts would be a better word or 'scarred little Smarians who had no choice' might be better way of putting it. The only way out of national service was for your family to be very rich, a council member or you could hide from the authorities for the rest of your life! As most didn't have the first two options and didn't want to take the third, the best advice was to keep your head down and do as you were told for the next year.

The commandant and his three officers were sitting in the officers' quarters drinking their rations of ale. That and the rations of the all the 'recruits' as they wouldn't need them as they were in 'training'! They sat on their comfortable armchairs with the high backs so that when they passed out due to overindulgence they could sleep it off in some form of comfort. Something that happened quite often! Their uniforms were a brownish shade of red loosely fitting for comfort, not style. Out here there was no one to impress so they just didn't bother! Only the stripes on the top-left hand side of their tunics gave away their rank. The more stripes, the better their rank! To be an officer, you had to come from a good family as an officer's rank was more generally bought by their fathers to keep them from the hardship of having to go through training and suffer the harshness of going out into the wilds of Topside. That and their mothers would nag their fathers into making sure that her little soldier come to no harm, whatever the cost! The thought of their wives making their lives a living nightmare if they didn't was enough to spend as much as needed! When they were told that Tega had returned, they wondered what was so important for him to come back so quickly after his last visit for rations. They ordered the soldier to bring him in.

Tega entered the officers' quarters. His uniform was almost the same but was covered in the red dust of the desert. He had no stripes as he was considered not worthy of any rank. Merely a lowly scout that was left to roam Topside and got fed and watered now and then, rather like a scorse. Useful but not valued very much. His greyish blue face looked old and tired with the years spent outside and his hands were like old scorse flesh. Hard and toughened. His eyes now matt black with age.

"And to what do we owe the pleasure of this unscheduled visit, Tega?" asked the commandant as he sipped away at his ale. Not for one minute offering a cup to Tega. Well, he wasn't an officer after all!

"Surely you don't need any more rations? Been having a party out there on your own, have you, and run out already?" he continued, laughing at his own comments.

The other officers thought best to join in the laughter as they didn't want to seem unamused at the commandant's jokey remarks.

"Ha-ha," replied Tega sarcastically, for he had no respect for these supposed superiors of his. "No! I merely came back to break the good news to you!"

"Oh?" enquired the commandant. "Well, I love good news. So much better than bad news, don't you know? Bad news always cause problems and we don't much care for problems, do we, chaps?" And started to chortle again closely followed by his band of upper-class chums.

He stopped laughing and once the others had cottoned on to this, he continued. "And what good news is that?"

"The good news that, you, sir, Mr Commandant, sir, will have to break to the Great One! The good news that another one has landed! I'm sure he will want to reward the Smarian that gives him this piece of good news, don't you?" Tega said with a big smile brimming across his face.

All their faces dropped at the same time. Tell the Great One that another had landed! A feeling of gloom filled the room as Tega gleefully began to tell them his story. They had thought Tega was suffering from Topside madness when he had begun to tell them about what he had seen. "Another one gone doolally!" they had thought, hoped for. For often, a scout had returned with ridiculous stories of seeing things falling from the sky or seeing places and things that had to have been 'made' by someone or something aeons ago. They were used to it and were about to pat him on the head and send him on his way with an "Of course, we will look into it" when Tega, knowing that this is what they would do, produced something that would make them change their minds. From his backpack he had produced an item like nothing they had seen before. It was the metallic object that Tega had picked up. They looked closely at the markings on it which were unlike anything that they had ever seen before. Four separate markings adorned the object with some smaller ones following on underneath. They were all of a uniform size but made no sense to them. They were certainly not something from the Smarian language, old or new. Tega had explained that it had fallen from the object as it crashed to the floor and he had braved the intense heat to retrieve it to verify his tale. Tega had been painfully aware of the commandant and his officers' reaction to such news as Hundrey had been sent away many times with a pat on the back when he had told them the same stories that he had told Tega. Tega had known that in order to be believed he would have to bring proof and this he had done. The officers all took it in turns to look closer and scrutinise the object. Each had a theory, all-be-it wrong, of what it might be so that they didn't look too stupid in front of the others.

"It could be part of the fence that got blown away in the wind!" Said one thoughtfully in a half-hearted attempt of explanation.

"Or it could be part of a sledge that was originally used to transport the base out here!" said another very unconvincingly.

As the object was passed around the room, it soon became clear to the commandant that, even though he didn't want to admit it, this was definitely something that should be reported back to the Great One. Indeed, he thought long and hard of any excuse at all not to tell the Great One. However, with the evidence in hand and not wanting to just ignore it in case there were painful consequences, he reluctantly came to the conclusion that it had to be reported. With that decided, he slumped back into his chair and announced his intentions. After a murmur of "Yes, of course" and "Good decision" as all good officers did if they didn't want to spend a night outside of the complex, the commandant got up, straightened his uniform and made his way back to his office to prepare a report for the Great One. Probably once he had sobered up though!

Tega had taken the chance to rest for a day and collect more rations before he headed back out to the object. By now, the news of what he had seen had spread throughout the base and the officers and recruits were all talking about it amongst themselves. None had approached Tega about it as after many years alone out in the wastelands, Tega had learnt to keep to himself and regarded everyone with suspicion. That plus the fact that everyone considered him as completely mad meant that whenever he did return to base, he was left alone. Wherever he went people would steer clear of him and talk behind his back. This suited Tega as he had no wish to converse with them anyway much preferring the company of a beer and a good meal. The base wasn't a place that Tega liked staying at for too long and he wanted to be on his way. The commandant had got his map of where the object was and Tega was anxious to return to keep an eye on it. It had been a week's trek back to the base and Tega, for some reason, wanted to return to the object as soon as possible. He wasn't sure why but something had told him that there was more to this object than what he'd seen. He didn't look back as the gates slammed shut behind him. There was more on his mind than the two idiots that were now making impolite gestures at him from the ramparts of the base. He turned quickly and stared back at them and immediately they vanished from the ramparts back to the safety of the base. Tega turned and laughed out loud. *Fools and cowards*, he thought as he marched away from the base.

The week's trek back to the object had been as arduous as the trip back to base but Tega had been anxious to get back. He didn't know why but he knew that it was important to get there. It was as if he knew he might miss something. Something of great importance but he didn't have any idea what. Just a gut feeling that he wasn't about to ignore. As he got further away from the base and closer to the landing area, he felt a strange sensation racing through his body. Part of him wanted to turn around and get as far away as possible but there was a much stronger feeling pushing him onwards. A little voice inside his head urging him on. Telling him that he must go on. It was so strong that he couldn't resist it and he didn't want to resist it as for some reason, he knew it was the right thing to do. Mind you, he was quite used to the voices in his head telling him things, the result of being on one's own for years, and he normally found them quite comforting. Except, of course, until he started to argue with them and wondering what it would be like to lose that argument! It was then that he knew that he'd been at Topside for too long! However, this time he knew the voices were right! He had to get there and find out what it was and why he felt so drawn to it.

The landing site was over the next hill. Before he reached the top, he hit the harsh desert floor and crawled up to the last few yards on his belly. Tega took out his binoculars and surveyed the area. Yes, it was still there all right but something was different. There seemed to be more of it than he remembered but he couldn't see what it was. He would have to go down the hill and get closer. Much closer! He approached it very cautiously through the rocks and plotted himself up what he thought was a safe distance away and raised his binoculars up towards the object. It was still there but this time there seemed to be different bits surrounding it.

"Must have fallen off when it landed," muttered Tega to himself, as he often did as there was no one else to talk to.

Past the main object was another larger object that wasn't there before. It looked surprisingly like the base camp that he had come from. A huge dome like structure with what looked like a massive door. A massive army of Smarians could be housed in there without a problem or was something else hiding within.

"What is that on the side?" He murmured again to himself. He adjusted his binoculars so that he could get a closer look at the objects.

"Amazing," he said as he looked closer for there on the side of the object were the same four markings as were on the piece that he had taken away to show the commandant. He looked around at the other objects and although he couldn't be sure he could see more markings on the other smaller objects. He would have to get closer. Crawling through the rocks, he slowly drew closer to the object, his gaze constantly on it. He wasn't sure why he was taking so much care as he approached the object for nothing was moving but still thought that it was a good idea. Tega found another spot behind some rocks and raised his binoculars again. Sure enough, there were more markings on the smaller objects surrounding the main metallic object. Some had the same four markings but others had different markings on them. They varied in size and shape but were obviously not random. They made no sense to Tega but he felt sure that the scientists at Below would be able to work out what they were and what, if anything, they meant. Tega now had a bit of a dilemma. Should he go closer to the objects to get a better look or should he wait for backup? Backup! He wondered what type of backup he would receive. A crack troop of soldiers and top scientists or more likely a bunch of no hopers that were just unlucky enough to be picked out. Whilst he was pondering upon what to do, he heard an almighty crack. He dived back amongst the rocks and took cover. Nothing. He gave it a few minutes before cautiously peering over the rocks and looking back towards the objects. At first he could see nothing to have made such a noise. It wasn't until he took a closer look at the main object with his binoculars that he saw it. The side of the main object had cracked and there appeared to be a huge bit hanging off in a peculiar way. He rubbed his eyes and put his binoculars back again to have a better look. Just as he was focusing on the bit hanging off, he started to see something crawling from what appeared to be inside the object. He rubbed his eyes again in disbelief. Dust, perhaps, or a trick of the light. He looked again. This time he could clearly see something crawling out of the object. It was a huge white machine of some kind. At least twenty times the size of him. It clambered out of the object in a peculiar manner and slowly crawled down the side of it until it hit the ground. Then Tega could see more clearly what it was. It had only what appeared to be two arms and two legs, unlike a Smarian who obviously had four arms, two legs and a tail to boot. It, too, had strange markings all over it. Moving very slowly but purposefully towards one of the objects outside the main object, it seemed to kneel very gingerly beside it. At this point, Tega's gaze was interrupted as another one crawled out from the same space. It was identical to the other one in every way. Same amount of arms and legs and no tail. It, too, moved over towards the object that the other one was kneeling beside.

I must get closer, thought Tega and did so very, very cautiously so as not to be detected by these massive, machine-like things. By now, Hundrey's stories were flowing through his brain. Were these machines made by the ancient ones that he had always talked about? They were definitely not like anything that he had seen or heard about before. He got closer and raised his binoculars again. Yes, they were covered with more marking like he had seen on the other objects. They moved very clumsily around as if not very stable. Like a baby taking its first few steps and not knowing to use its tail for balance. For the first time, he could see what he thought were big glass bowls where the heads should be. The machines had been facing away from him so he had gotten quite close now. On the back of the machines were like huge backpacks with pipes going directly into the bowl-like heads of the machines. They had both been looking at the object on the floor but now one of them had turned its bulbous head and, although not looking directly at Tega, he could see inside the glass bowl for the first time. He was astounded at what he saw.

"That can't be!" he said to himself a little louder than he would have liked. "No! How can that be?"

Chapter 2
The Landing

The doors to the Great Chamber were just minutes away. The Herald, whilst knowing he had to do it, was full of anxiety for the task that lay ahead of him. Yes, the Great One had demanded to know if and when another ever came. Yes, He had been adamant that He wanted to know as soon as it happened, if it ever happened again. Yes, He had barked at everyone at that meeting with His booming voice, banging His desk hard with His fists to emphasise just how important it was that He be told immediately, should this ever happen again. The clerics and the scientists all agreeing that He would be the first to know but all hoping that it never did. For none wanted to have to break the news to Him if it did. The Herald was none too keen either to be the one that had to tell the Great One that another had actually arrived. However, the clerics and the scientists had all agreed that, in the interests of science and all things holy, it would be him. The real reason being that they outranked him and were scared of having to do it themselves. The thought of standing in front of the Great One and having to break the news that another one had the audacity to land on Smar yet again was, indeed, a very disturbing one. The Herald's footsteps slowed and his heart rate dropped as the doors, those huge, ornate, heavy doors that led to the Great Chamber came into view. A sense of foreboding came over the Herald as he approached the entrance. His head slowly dropping and disappearing into his neck with fear.

The last time it happened, the Great One went into such a rage. For weeks, He was in such a foul mood. Blaming everyone but Himself, naturally, for the arrival of the thing. The clerics for not foretelling Him before it had arrived and the scientists for not telling Him *why* it had arrived! Then, as was the norm when no one wanted to admit that it might have possibly been ever so slightly their fault, everyone started blaming everyone else. The clerics blamed the scientists for it was an unholy thing and, therefore, was nothing that they could surely foretell. The scientists blamed the clerics for as it was not from this world then surely it had to be from the heavens and out of their jurisdiction. Each blamed the other, no matter what argument was thrown up from the other side, and there had been plenty of arguments. This infuriated the Great One even more until one of the clerics, rather stupidly thought all the others actually had the audacity to suggest that someone should go Topside and see exactly what it was. A bit miffed that He had not thought of it first, the Great One dismissed the idea out of hand for a least an hour or so. The arguments raged on until the Great One came up with exactly the same idea proclaiming it as His own. Without thinking, the cleric that had originally thought of it chirped up that it was exactly what he had said earlier and then immediately regretted saying it as soon as he had. For as a 'thank you' as he thought it was HIS idea, he would be sent on an expedition to the desolate, cruel, desert known as Topside. Anyone else that didn't agree or had a better idea, not that they could as after all He was the Great One, was also included on this "fantastic chance to see Topside first-hand" as He put it. Indeed even the Herald thought himself as 'lucky' not to be sent on the expedition himself to find out exactly what it was as he had been the one to tell the Great One in the first place. *Very lucky*, he thought as only a few made it back from the journey to Topside and even fewer ever found out exactly what it was.

Despite much speculation, the Great Council, who had 'all' the facts, had decreed that it was nothing but a rock from the sky and that was an end to it. However there had been rumours. Rumours of a great machine that roamed the surface looking for something. Moving around the surface searching for weeks until it just…stopped! Rumours that it had been taken to THE place and hidden away from all but the Great Council and a few 'lucky' scientists and clerics that were never seen or heard of again. Rumours that had of course been put down by the Great Council and anyone caught printing such things in the newspapers had had a visit from the 'Information Bureau' and had been persuaded, for want of a better word, not to print any more for the good of the Smarian people and themselves, 'OR ELSE'. The 'OR ELSE' seemed to be the main persuasive point as anyone found not following the Great Council protocol could be deemed a traitor. This would result into an immediate loss of public standing, which no family member, especially the wife, would allow as well as a long spell Topside which no one wanted. Or, they might just one day disappear without trace. No questions asked or dared to be for not wanting to suffer the same fate.

But this time it was different. This time it was bigger, much bigger.

The guards to the Great Chamber had seen him coming and were slowly opening the huge doors for him. They were dressed in the Smarians finest uniforms. Their bright red tunics all neatly cleaned and pressed with sparkling gold braid around the cuffs and collars. Unearned medals adorning their chests. A little tight around the midriff which was being held in by the thick belt with the bright gold buckle taking the strain. Their whiter than white trousers dressed off with the shiniest of boots. Definitely not the kind of uniforms any of the other unfortunate soldiers got to wear. For these were the Great One's personal guards. Actually they were the Great One's two nephews. His big sister had threatened all kinds of unpleasant things if He had sent them Topside to do their national service. None of which were repeatable and all of which He believed she would do as she had proved all through their childhood. They were incompetent but anything for an easy life!

The Herald nodded his reluctant appreciation as he passed through into the Great Chamber. The doors slammed shut behind him once he had passed through and he knew then that there was no escape now as he continued on his way.

Inside the Great Chamber was filled with great splendour. Portraits of the past 'Great Ones' adorned the walls all around. Their eyes seemed to follow you everywhere you went and the Herald always thought that they were scolding him for something. He was quite used to that feeling with the current 'Great One' so just assumed that it was part of their job. To make others feel incompetent and small and he, for one, was very good at feeling that way around most people actually. He carried on towards the Great One not daring to look up until he got there or was spoken to. Because of this, he had, over the years, got to know the big red carpet that ran from one end of the chamber to the other very well. It was the first thing that he saw when he cowered into the chamber and the last thing he saw as he cowered back out again. He sometimes wondered if he actually knew what was in the great chamber other than the carpet, the pictures that followed him everywhere, the big desk at the end and the Great One Himself! *Funny what goes through your head when you're scared*, he thought as he continued further into the chamber.

There at the end of the chamber behind the huge, finely polished, ornately carved, regal looking desk on an equally huge leather backed, ornately carved, regal looking chair, sat the Great One. His head was buried in a pile of what must be very important paperwork as He was a very important person or so He thought. The fact that He had been dozing and had only awoken upon hearing the doors creak open and slam shut was neither here nor there. No one would question Him as He was after all the Great One. Seeing that the Herald was now almost at His desk he shuffled some papers and looked up over the top of his wired rimmed glasses that hung dangerously close to end of His nose. He liked doing this as He considered it made him look more important.

"Well?" He barked at the Herald who it was apparent didn't want to be there. "Why have you disturbed me whilst I am trying to read these important papers? It had better be a good reason. Good news, I hope, as I loathe and detest bad news. Gives me indigestion, you know. The last time you gave me bad news, I couldn't eat properly for a week. Very disconcerting. Well, what's it to be? Spit it out, man!"

The Herald made a noise. Not a large noise. More of a whimper. Actually not quite even a whimper more of a...noise!

"Can't understand a thing you said. Get a grip. What have you come in here for?" The Great One shuffled some more paper to make it look as if He was busy and then looked back up at the Herald and demanded, very loudly, "What is it?"

Seeing that the Great One was now getting a bit upset, the Herald pulled himself up straight, cleared his throat and blurted out, "There's been another one sighted on the surface!"

Amazed that he had actually found the courage to say it, the Herald almost had a wry smile on his face until he saw the look on the Great One's face and thought better of it.

This bold announcement seemed to stop the Great One in His tracks. The papers that he'd been shuffling just slipped from His hands and found a place on His desk to stop in no apparent order. This would normally have angered the Great One as He hated disorder but this time, it was He who was having trouble finding His words. Indeed, His jaw had dropped and there was a stunned silence. The Great One slowly fell back into His chair. The remaining papers left in His hands made a break for the floor and fell like leaves dropping from a poslethwaite tree in the months of llaf.

The Great One was true to His name as He was rather a rotund being. His belly was the result of far too many 'working lunches' and 'necessary banquets' and 'working breakfasts, afternoon teas, coffee mornings...' The list was endless but all very necessary! It was fortunate that the people of Smar had been blessed with four arms as he would never be able to keep pace with holding so much food and drink

25

with just two arms. His tail also helped keep him upright when the Smarian ale flowed just a little too much. A necessary thing sometimes, of course! His face was slightly bluer in the cheeks and nose than others. A sign that the endless rich food and wine had been flowing a little too much! His glasses hung at the end of His small nose and His bulbous black eyes were peering over them. He was dressed in the finest of clothes as only a Great One should be. Very similar to the guards except that His tunic was a light blue with even more unearned medals. His belt was wider as it had more to hold in and the gold buckle was much more ornate. His boots shone from all the polishing that someone else had lovingly put into them. Around His huge neck hung the chain of office that lets everyone know that He was the Great One! He was also wearing rather large gaudy gold rings on every finger. No one could say that He didn't at least look the part not that anyone dare say otherwise anyway.

The Herald was still cowering on the spot rather awkwardly. He had been expecting the Great One to bellow at him but that hadn't happened…yet! Unlike the Great One, the Herald was quite small in stature. He had the customary four arms and a tail but his belly had not had to 'put up' with all those banquets, etc. His clothes again similar. His tunic red like the guards but with no medals and a rather old, worn-out kind of belt pulled the tunic together. The boots too had seen better days and had more of a dim look to them rather than a shine. He himself was generally a nervous being because he was the one that always had to bring the news to the Great One, be it good or bad. He was used to being shouted at and that only made him more nervous as he expected it every time he went into the Great Chamber. A quivering wreck would be

26

a more suitable description of him and one wondered why he stayed in the job. Probably because he was more afraid of telling his wife that he really wanted to be a poet and not a bureaucrat. Oh, how he wanted to just spend his days writing poems of love and beauty, rather than pushing paperwork around and taking the news to the Great One. But she would have none of this nonsense. No, better to be a Smarian who talks to the Great One every day than a no-good poet! What would the neighbours think? Her family and friends would never understand and she would certainly never be able to go to the Smarian Women of the Year awards as the wife of a poet! What about her position in the community? Their children, her ego…hence he stayed a Herald!

By now, the Great One was beginning to make some kind of audible noise. Looking bemused, the Herald stopped cowering and leant towards the Great One. With a start, the Great One leapt to Hs feet and banged the table with all four of His fists letting out a mighty roar. The Herald leapt backwards and took up his usual professional cowering position.

"Is it the same as the last one?" demanded the Great One leaning over His desk inquisitively as if, in other words, the reply should be, "No, nothing like it!"

"Er…no, oh, Great One." replied the Herald uncurling himself so to speak.

The Great One was about to give a sigh of relief before the Herald continued.

"This one is different. It's…it's…" hesitated the Herald trying hard to get the words out.

"It's what!!!" shouted the Great One, getting rather agitated again.

"It's…it's much, much bigger!" continued the Herald and immediately resumed his cowering position.

The Great One sank back into his seat. There was a moment's silence before He said, rather slowly and in a menacing way, "Get me the General!"

The General was in, well, what he thought, was his big important office down the hallway from the Great Chamber. *Not quite as big as the Great Chamber but much bigger and grander*, he thought, than the other council members. To get to him, the Herald had to first get past his secretary. She, who thought that as the General's secretary, she was more important than anyone else and acted like it too! The Herald hated her as she made him almost as nervous as the Great One did. As he walked towards the General's office, he thought this time it will be different. This time he will barge in and demand to speak to the General as, after all, he had been sent by the Great One himself. His mind made up, he swung open the door, walked straight in, looked the secretary straight in the eye and…froze!

The secretary, Mildread to her friends to which there were very few, looked up over her large, gaudy, bejewelled framed spectacles and, like a school ma'am, looked the Herald up and down. She looked every bit a school ma'am. She wore a white blouse with red buttons and a fancy collar set off by a black tight skirt. Her fuller figure making all her clothes look somewhat tight! *Her icy made-up white face and red lips with just a little too much blue blusher on her cheeks made her face look a tad scary*, thought the Herald.

Placing her pen slowly back down on the desk in a way that let everyone know that she was not someone to be trifled with, she spoke. "Lost your manners?" she enquired in her cold-hearted authoritarian voice, not expecting an answer. The Herald could only stand there blubbering something totally intelligible like a naughty schoolboy caught doing something he really shouldn't be doing.

"Most people knock before they enter a room. It's only polite. Now go outside and come back in again but knock this time," she said, promptly pointing towards the door.

The Herald started to protest but was cut short with a masterful "OUT!"

He was now standing outside leaning up against the door wondering what had happened to his plan of marching in and demanding to see the General. Before he had time to reconcile his situation, a voice from inside the office demanded, "Well, are you coming in or not?"

Obediently the Herald knocked, walked in and asked, very politely, if it was at all possible at the bequest of the Great One, to speak to the General. What passed for a smile, or more probably a contented inner feeling of dominance over the little runt of a Herald, appeared from the secretary as she slowly responded with a very polite, "I will check for you."

The General was snoozing quietly when the intercom woke him with a start. He immediately started shuffling some important papers before he realised that no one was actually in the room. Bemused, he looked around wondering what had woken him when the intercom buzzed again.

"What is it? Don't you know I'm busy?" barked the General.

His secretary, in a polite but firm voice, explained that the Herald was here with a message from the Great One.

The General thought for a moment. If it was anyone else he would have dismissed them out of hand unless of course they had a good reason to be there. Lunch perhaps or a dinner invitation. Drinks in the bar! However, a message from the Great One, he couldn't ignore. Perhaps it was a lunch invitation after all! The General sat up straight and switched on the intercom. "Hmm. Better send him in then."

The secretary removed her finger from the intercom, turned towards the Herald and beckoned him into the office. The Herald walked into the office, thanking the secretary through gritted teeth as he passed her.

The General was also a somewhat rotund person as he, too, had to attend the same amount of the necessary banquets, etc. as the Great One did. Indeed, sometimes they were the only ones there so had to make up for all of the others that weren't! His office had many pictures of him with other important people at important places doing important things. Medals were strategically placed so that they could be seen by anyone who walked in, assuring them that he was a very important person. He always wore his best uniform, just in case. Very similar to everyone else but a strange shade of puce. His choice apparently but no one ever commented on it. Well, not whilst he could hear them anyway! In case of what he didn't know but just in case!

"What is it?" growled the General, knowing that he made the Herald feel uneasy in doing so. It amused the General but terrified the Herald.

The Herald spoke quietly yet quite confidently. After all, he had already told the Great One!

"There's been another landing and the Great One requests your presence in the Great Chamber immediately to explain why he wasn't informed of this before it happened!"

He hadn't but the Herald's only source of enjoyment was making the General jump to attention at the thought of the Great One demanding his presence about something he knew nothing about. He had a little snigger to himself as the General started to flap about shouting for his secretary to make sure that he looked smart for the Great One. The secretary was well used to this and as usual tried her best to assure the General that he looked fantastic and should be on his way. As they both left the office, the General, in front, still flapping about with the Herald, following just behind, the secretary glared at the Herald with a 'I'll get you for this' kind of glare. The Herald smiled back at her with a "Ha!"

The General ran as fast as he could which wasn't fast at all as he was quite a lazy Smarian really. His short, fat little arms and hands waving around crazily as if by this method he would actually go faster which wasn't really happening. His fat little body waddled from side to side in time with his arms making him look absolutely ridiculous. His tail flaying around trying desperately to balance his seriously wobbling blob of a body. A lot of movement in all directions except forwards! For a General, or indeed anyone, he was completely unfit and had justified this to himself and anyone else who would listen, by saying that he just didn't have the time to defend the Smarian people and keep in good shape. After all, what was the point of having all those troops to do the hard work and be fit yourself? No! Better he spent more time refining the efficiency of his masterful, tactical mind than wasting it on honing his fat overweight body! No general ever won a battle running around on the battlefield! No, a general won battles by staying back where it was safe and sound whilst using the troops to do the dirty work and see if his tactics worked. If his tactics worked, then all would be in wonderment of his superior brain and if it didn't…well, there's always more troops! The Herald, on the other hand, was used to running around everywhere so to follow the General at his pace was quite leisurely. The hallway from the General's office to the Great Chamber was quite long and the Herald often used this time to make up a poem or two depending on how fast the General was waddling that day. Sometimes he thought he might make up a complete novel if the pace was unusually slow. His mind began to wander as they made their way to the Great Chamber.

I wander lonely as a scorse is right, that floats high o'er mountain and desert, whereupon I feast my eyes upon on a host of… thought the Herald to himself as they approached the Great Chamber, trying to quickly write it down before he forgot it completely.

This time, the guards stood to attention and saluted the General with the customary salute. This meant their top right and left hands raised and the thumbs pressed to the side of their heads. The other three fingers of each hand were fanned out to resemble something like antlers. Their other hands pressed closely to their side, feet together. A bizarre salute but they took such pride in it. The General acknowledged their salute with a half-hearted attempt of his own as he bustled past them into the Great Chamber. The Herald followed him in and the guards closed the doors. They hurriedly made their way along the familiar red carpet to the other end of the chamber where the Great One was awaiting them. They stopped just in front of the desk and waited for the Great one to say something. The General's body still seemed to be moving in all directions as if dancing and having a good time even though they'd stopped moving!

"Well?" spoke the Great One looking at the General squarely in his eyes. The General was about to say that he was, in fact, very well and hoped that the Great One was in good health too but before he spoke and made a fool of himself, the Great One continued, "It seems as if they've come back and bigger this time. What do you intend to do about it?"

The General shuffled around uncomfortably raising his hand as if to say something only to lower it whilst muttering to himself. He hadn't stopped to think that the Great One actually wanted him to DO anything about it. Indeed he had rather hoped that the Great One was going to tell him what to do about it! This obviously wasn't the case so he waffled on a bit hoping that something would enter his head and save the day.

"Well we could ignore it and hope it goes away or..." he said quickly as he could see that was not what the Great One wanted to hear "...or we could send some troops up there to spy on them and see what it's doing?" he finished his sentence rather as a question than a statement from a brilliant tactician.

This met with a much better reaction from the Great One and the General relaxed a bit.

"Ah! Yes, we could do that, couldn't we?" replied the Great One thinking as he said it. "Dangerous job, though. We would have to be very careful who we send as we have no idea what dangers await them. Remember the last time!"

"Of course, sir," said the somewhat relieved General trying not to remember the disastrous last encounter on Topside. Something that he had tried not to remember for years. Just how many soldiers did they lose in that encounter?

"I could send some of my best men to…"

"NO!"

The General jumped back as he was cut short by the Great One.

"We don't want to risk sending the best men for this job. What if they all got killed…or worse?"

"Hmm," they said in unison and both held their chins as if in deep thought whilst the confused Herald was trying to work out what exactly was worse than being killed! A weekend with his wife's family locked away on a desert island perhaps…or a whole week! He physically shook with the thought of it.

"No," the Great One said with a wry smile appearing on his face. The General, too, began to smile without knowing why but deciding that it was probably the safer option than looking quizzical.

"We lost too many last time. This time it will be different. This time you will find some 'volunteers' that we can afford to lose or someone that we really don't mind losing!" Then with a big grin on his face, he said, "Who was that idiot that survived last time and tried to tell everyone all about it? You know, the one that went to the press just before we rewarded him by sending him away to the North on a 'research' mission?"

"Ah…ah!" It had now dawned on the General what the Great One was saying. "You mean Sergeant Ha'an?" More a question again than a reply.

"Yes!" The Great One replied, realising that the penny had eventually dropped with the General.

"…and he can take some of the new recruits doing their national service. Don't want to waste good money on training them if they're not going to come back now, do we?"

"Certainly not," agreed the General feeling much happier that the Great One wasn't asking him to go Topside. A terrifying thought that had crossed his mind for an instance and given him palpitations. No one wants to go Topside!

"Get your secretary to get a list of the 'lucky' individuals together this afternoon and then get someone else to get the men ready to leave tonight. No point prolonging their lives, er, hmm…opportunity to serve the Smarian nation now is there?" the Great One correcting himself almost immediately. "Best we find out exactly what's happening up there. Providing one of them returns, of course. Ha-ha. If not…well er, we'll just have to send someone else, won't we?" and with that the Great One leaned menacingly towards the General as if to let him know that HE would be the next 'lucky' candidate.

"I'll get my secretary on it straight away."

The Herald just sighed for he had seen this happen before. Who would be the unlucky volunteers for this one-way trip? He just stood there not uttering a word whilst the Great One and the General laughed and congratulated themselves on such a good plan.

"Well, now that that's resolved…how about a spot of lunch?" enquired the Great One looking at his watch and already knowing the answer.

"A good idea, sir. All that thinking has given me quite an appetite. Usual restaurant, on expenses of course?" asked the General. He, too, already knew the answer.

"Of course. Can't be doing all that hard work for the good of the nation without getting some kind of reward for it now, can we?"

And with that they both started to laugh again. Putting their arms around each other, well as best they could, they walked towards the door discussing what they were going to eat and just how many courses they thought they deserved. The Herald rushed in front of them and opened the door bowing courteously as they passed then following on behind them. He had to go too. Not to indulge in the food and drink. No, he had to sign the expenses slip!

Chapter 3
The Team

The commandant strutted into the small room where the others were waiting. A storm was raging outside and the wind and dust were battering the walls of the domed complex and making a colossal amount of noise. Not an uncommon event for Topside! Inside the room stood two of his officers guarding the four willing 'volunteers' who were sitting on one of the benches in this rather drab, grey-looking room. Well actually they weren't willing. Rather they had no choice in the matter. They were the misfits of the platoon and the most disliked of all amongst the recruits for one reason or another so no one had any problem with 'volunteering' them. Plus they had been 'volunteered' by the officers as well! No one in their right mind would volunteer to go out of the complex on such a mission, any mission, and certainly not during a storm!

"Ah," started the commandant. "so these are my brave volunteers." He looked at the four disgruntled, dismayed and dejected recruits. *Good! Not the 'best men' then*, he thought to himself.

Just as one of the 'volunteers' was about to protest his reluctance to take part, a sharp jab from one of the officers sticks in the back put paid to his objection.

"Good to see that there are brave recruits amongst our young Smarians these days," he continued ignoring the groans of the 'volunteer' as he winced from being hit.

"As you know, this is a very important mission and the Great One himself has personally asked to be kept informed. You were chosen by your fellow recruits and officers as they all felt that you were the best qualified to take on this dangerous and heroic mission."

The commandant thought it best to 'big-up' the recruits before they were about to take on something that they weren't expected to survive or come back from. Give them hope as they were going to need it!

"You will leave tonight with Sergeant Ha'an and find out exactly what it is that Tega saw. Any questions?"

Not expecting any, the commandant turned and started to walk away when one of the recruits shouted out before an officer could get to him, "I have a question!"

The commandant, rather surprised and disgruntled, stopped in his tracks. Slowly turning around and putting a false smile on his face, he looked at the recruits one at a time. Once establishing just who had dared ask a question, he marched towards the recruit.

"What is it?" asked the commandant in a very polite manner but through gritted teeth. He wasn't used to people asking questions, merely just blindly following his orders.

"There's a storm outside. Wouldn't it be more prudent to wait until it blew over?" questioned the recruit rather hopefully.

"Prudent, yes." replied the commandant rather agreeably raising the recruit's hopes before completely dashing them with, "However, you're in the Smarian army now, boy.

Prudent isn't a word we use. You leave tonight!" And with that, the commandant turned and marched out the room as quickly as he could before anyone else could say anything. The door slammed behind him and any hope of a reprieve walked out with him.

With the four recruits now left without any hope at all of escaping this mission, the two officers proceeded to usher the 'volunteers' out of the room with their sticks and marched them down the corridor to the supply room, giving extra whacks to the recruit who had been stupid enough to ask a question. There, they would meet Sergeant Ha'an. Unfortunately for them, he wasn't going to be exactly what they expected or hoped for either! He too didn't openly volunteer for this mission. More had to be dragged, kicking and screaming, from his bunk by two hefty guards to the supply room after being told that the Great One had given him the great honour of leading this expedition! Screams of "Why me?" and "Kill me now!" had to be stifled from him along the way until he very reluctantly and knowing that he had no other option, had accepted his fate!

He was a rather nervous character to say the least. He had jumped as they burst into the room and was now on the floor clumsily picking up his supplies that he had dropped, muttering to himself about how this couldn't be happening to him again. His uniform was slightly too big for him and he was wearing very thick spectacles. Ha'an wasn't the biggest of people and certainly wasn't the fittest. Normally someone of his age would be back below but the council had seen fit to keep Ha'an at Topside. He was as far away from a professional, well-trained soldier as you could ever expect anyone to be. Indeed, he almost made the four volunteers look competent and that wasn't an easy task!

One of the officers approached Ha'an, patted him on the back and said, "These are your volunteers for the mission. Be sure to bring them all back as we've spent a lot of time training them. Well, two weeks anyway!"

Both the officers laughed as they made their way out of the room. Just as they were about to go one of them turned around and said, "See you at the main gate in thirty minutes," and then departed, still laughing.

The room fell silent. The volunteers looked at Ha'an, then at each other and then back at Ha'an. A feeling of total disbelief and impending doom had filled the room. It was as if all hope had walked out of the room with the two officers, not that there had been much to begin with. Ha'an looked at his team. All were very young and apprehensive just as he had been when he first arrived at the complex. He could tell that none of them wanted to be there but, as with him, had no choice. Pulling himself up from the floor, he dusted himself off and straightened his uniform as best he could and introduced himself.

"I am Sergeant Ha'an," he started. "And we are heading out to meet scout Tega, near the landing site, where we will ascertain exactly what it is that we are dealing with."

Feeling a bit more confident after he had managed to introduce himself without breaking down and sobbing, "I want to go home," he continued. "Now, let's see who we have here."

He walked towards the first recruit.

"What's your name, son?"

"My name is Karel, sir!" said the young recruit standing slightly to attention. He was very tall and very thin. His uniform was clean and tidy but just a little short in the arm and leg regions. The lad seemed keen to impress which made Ha'an feel a bit better about himself. Most people just laughed at him or ignored him, no matter what rank they were. He had long been the butt of many a joke even though he was the sole survivor of the previous, notorious landing mission.

"I just wanted to ask whether we know what it is we're doing out there, sir. How long will we be gone and just how much danger will we face? Are we meeting anyone else out there or is it just us? If it's just us, will that be enough? I mean we're new and can't possibly be expected to do it alone, can we? How far are we going anyway? Will we need a scorse? Who's going to look after it…"

Karel continued with his barrage of questions whilst Ha'an just looked at him in amazement. Not a breathe was taken during this continual torrent of questions that erupted from boy.

I think I know why he was volunteered, thought Ha'an.

Karel was still in full flow when Ha'an placed his hand over Karel's mouth to stop him. As Ha'an removed his hand, Karel started up again and Ha'an placed his hand back a bit harder.

"Hush now. No more questions. Understand?"

Karel nodded and Ha'an slowly removed his hand. Boy, this recruit could talk!

Ha'an looked him up and down as if knowing what he was looking for, he didn't but he was banking on them not knowing that and moved onto the next recruit.

"And you are?"

"Name's Krun, sir," said the second recruit, who was also standing to attention. Much like the first but smaller, this one had a cheeky smile on his face that didn't seem to show any realisation of the extent of danger that they were about to face.

"Why are you smiling?" Enquired Ha'an. "Do you have any idea of where we are about to go and the danger that we will be in?"

"Always smile, sir. No matter where I am or what the circumstances. Come from the far east of Below, sir. Where the Scorse are bred, sir. If you get miserable there, sir, you might as well top yourself. So my mum and dad said that I should always find the positive side of any situation, smile and make the best of things, sir. Been doing it all my life, sir. Was glad to get to Topside for a change of scenery and some fresh air, sir."

Glad to be on Topside! That was a first, thought Ha'an, *never met anyone who was glad to be at Topside nor someone who was so damn happy to be there! Did he not realise the imminent danger that they were in or did he just not care? Topside was not the kind of place to be happy!*

Mind you, Ha'an had never been to the east where the scorse were bred and had he might have thought different!

Now the scorse were the source of all power for the Smarian people at Below. Huge, great, long, worm like creatures with numerous amounts of legs depending on their age and size. They had two eyes on either side of their head, a nose and a large mouth. Their skin was a greyish blue colour, not unlike that of the Smarian people, which was thick and leathery but smooth to the touch. They weren't the most intelligent of creatures but the Smarians had realised that they had one saving grace. You see, the scorse had a great capacity to create…gas! Yes, feed them anything and within minutes, they farted! The gas was so explosive that the Smarian people had aeons ago learnt, after a few, well quite a few, disastrous mishaps, to domesticate the scorse and harness their rather noxious bi-product and powered the whole of Below with it. They used it to power everything from vehicles to the streetlights. Homes and industries relied on these creatures for their everyday power. Scorse were found outside every household and office building, every restaurant and bar. Wherever power was needed, there would be a scorse somewhere. Just hook it up to a generator, feed it and BINGO! Instant free power! There were even scorse stations where anyone could just pull up, hook up their vehicle, feed a scorse and fuel up for the journey. Very convenient for the Smarians but not so good for the scorse. But as luck would have it, the scorse seemed content enough providing that they were being fed. After all, they didn't really have to do much. Just what came naturally! Well, that was what the council told everyone and as they were all only too pleased to have the power, no one seemed too concerned about the scorses. There was the occasional 'Scorse rites' activists but no one paid them too much attention. They were just allowed to rant and rave in their small groups in the town centres as much as they liked until they got bored or their megaphone ran out of power. With no scorse to power it back up again, they usually gave up and went home. Confident that they had done their bit for the scorses. The scorses, of course, were completely unaware of what they had done nor really cared. They just continued eating and farting! For one month of the year, most of the scorses were all herded together for breeding in the east and some unfortunate people, like Krun, had to look after them. The smell was something that you definitely didn't want to become accustomed to. Indeed, during that month there would be so much gas produced from the mating season that it had to be released out from below to topside to stop the whole place from blowing up! A waste of gas but a big relief to the noses of all who had to live there!

Ha'an looked at the third who, for some reason, wasn't standing to attention. He was sitting down.

"Get up," demanded Ha'an and up and up and up he got! The room seemed to get a lot smaller and darker the further UP he got! He was enormous! In all directions! Ha'an and the other recruits all backing away to make space as he expanded to fill the room. His uniform looked as if it was made from a tent...or two! His hands were bigger than dinner plates and his powerful arms were thicker than most Smarians legs! In all, he was a VERY BIG lad!

"I'm Athan Sergeant," said this hulk of a Smarian in a kind of shy, quiet, deep voice almost as if he was ashamed of his height and build. His eyes looked down at the floor as a scolded child would but just who on Smar would have the courage to scold him!

Ha'an had backed up right to the wall as Athan had 'got up' and was now adjusting his glasses to make sure that his eyes weren't playing tricks on him. *Nope*, he thought, *he was definitely a very, very big lad! Just how did he get through the door?*

"Well," Ha'an said nervously trying to regain his composure. "It's...it's very nice to meet you." Trying not to sound intimidated or scared even though the expression on his face gave him away, he continued, "Pl...pl...please sit down again. There's a good chap," more pleading with him than asking!

And with that, Athan started his descent bringing light back into the room. They all breathed a sigh of relief as he landed back on the bench.

Ha'an moved along the wall trying to act casual with his eyes fixed firmly on Athan until he was standing in front of the fourth and last recruit. This one was looking at the floor and paying no attention at all to what was going on around him and mumbling to himself incoherently. He was the shortest of them all, which was a bit of a relief after Athan, and quite well rounded. He too sported glasses that had obviously seen better days. His uniform fitted him only in the places that it could reach, allowing his underwear to peek through rather disturbingly. In ways, he looked a bit like a mini Ha'an.

"Hello!" said Ha'an in a sarcastic way after gathering his composure.

"Oh," said the recruit. "Sorry but you see I shouldn't be here. The guy that was picked pushed me forward when the officer turned away so you see..."

"What's your name?" Ha'an cut him short.

"My name? Yes! It's Dez, sir. Short for Dezeremella."

"Well, Dez short for Dezeremella, none of us want to be here," he said. "Me, especially! But we have no choice! Trust me I know!" continued Ha'an, unreassuringly. "My only hope is that we can stick together and then perhaps, perhaps we might make it back. I hope. I mean I really hope that we can make it back!"

Dez didn't look convinced. Why should he? Ha'an was trying desperately to convince himself and he didn't believe it either!

"Now let's get our equipment together and make our way to the gates. Let's leave this complex at least looking as though we're soldiers on an important mission for the Great One!"

Filled with no confidence whatsoever, they began in silence to gather their equipment together.

Ha'an was checking everything twice just in case he had forgotten anything. He hadn't been the same since his first close encounter with things that fell from the sky. He still had nightmares of things landing on him, hence his nervous disposition. This wasn't helped by his fellow officers taking it in turns to drop things on his head whilst he was asleep and watching and laughing as Ha'an ran around screaming the place down and shouting, "They're back!"

When the commandant had called him into his office, he had been told that he was the 'best man for the job', because of his experiences but he had thought that it was yet another attempt to get rid of him. He wasn't far from wrong!

Backpacks on and reluctantly they all walked slowly across the empty enclosed parade ground towards the main gate. The wind didn't seem to be making as much noise now, not that any of them had noticed. They were all too wrapped up in their own worlds. Trying hard not to think too much of what was waiting for them somewhere out on Topside. Not knowing or wanting to know of how the coming events in the next few weeks would change their lives and the lives of everyone on Smar forever.

There weren't any other signs of life within the dome. Everyone else was tucked up warm and safe in their beds. Gently dreaming of their families and friends back down at Below. Only the two gate guards and one of the officers were standing there waiting for them.

"Well, you'll be pleased to know that the storm is subsiding so you won't get lost just outside the complex," he said sarcastically. "Make sure that you radio in every day with a progress report."

Ha'an nodded a rather half-hearted nod.

Report in, indeed, he thought, *report in so as to make sure we haven't tried to run away, you mean! Just where do they think we'd run away to?*

The officer beckoned to the guards, who then began to open the main gate. It slowly creaked open revealing the uninviting storm-swept desert. The storm had indeed died down as they ventured out through the gate into the darkness. Ha'an checked his compass and pointed forward. Off in a line, they went into the vast openness of the unforgiving desert that was Topside. The main gate shut behind them, with a large bang. Dez looked back to see the domed complex for what he thought might be the last time. Their adventure was just beginning!

Chapter 4

The Storm

The dark sky of night, with its blanket of glittering stars that shone brightly with the light from a distant and long ago past and the blue star that looked so close that you might reach it someday, had slowly relented and transformed into the bright red sky of morning. The sun looked so close that you thought that you might feel its warmth but that certainly wasn't the case as the cold bit deep into their bodies. Now they could see the awesome, vast and desolate red landscape that surrounded them. During the night, all they could really see through the darkness was the shadows that danced in their lamplight. Shadows that would let the dark side of their imagination run wild with speculation as to what and who was out there watching and waiting for them. Shadows that brought no joy but added to their dread and fear. Except for Krun, of course! He thought it great the way the shadows danced and smiled his way through the night! He was the Ying to everyone else's Yang! With the daylight, the realisation of their predicament became apparent. They really were alone in this silent, deadly desert. They had no point of reference as the base was now well out of sight and, all around them, the nothingness of the desert with only the mountains on the horizon to break up the monotonous landscape. Rocks of all different shapes and sizes were scattered everywhere. Some, they had to walk around as they were so big. Others just lay in the red dust where they had probably laid for a millennium. This truly was a landscape that time had forgotten. The only time that it faced a change of any kind was when the frequent mighty storms blew across the wastelands. The sheer velocity of the wind whipping up the dust and the rocks and moving all that lay in its path. Something that they were very soon about to experience first-hand for themselves!

They had walked through the night across the desert towards the mountains. Ha'an in front, with his compass guiding the way, stopping every now and again, taking a bearing, pointing onwards and then continuing. Well, that was what it looked like he was doing anyway and the others seemed convinced so he continued to do it. No need to tell them that from the moment they had left the compound that Ha'an was just going in the same direction that the officer had told him to go. Hoping upon all hope that it wasn't just another one of their cruel jokes! And as for taking a bearing, well, he couldn't see anything to take a bearing from! Dez was bringing up the rear with their scorse on a lead. They had to have a scorse to power the equipment and Dez had been assigned to look after it. Mainly because Krun thought that they should release it and let it enjoy its freedom and Karel just came up with so many questions as what to do with it that Ha'an decided very quickly that was not a good idea either! Ha'an didn't give it to Athan as they were all afraid that he might sit on it or worse…eat it!

It was quite a young small scorse as they didn't need much power but still quite a smelly creature. Dez was quite happy to be considered for any form of responsibility as he was normally used to being overlooked. He was also very pleased that the wind was blowing in the right direction!

Ha'an had spent his time thinking about what he had really done so bad so as to be stranded out on Topside yet again! Surely after years of silence he had proved that he could be trusted with the truth. Okay! He had blabbed to that snoopy, yet very pretty, journalist about their mission to the surface last time. Yes, he had told her about what he saw and about the Smarians they lost to that unstoppable, monstrous machine from the sky. Sure, he had told her about all the things that he shouldn't have about 'THE' place but was that any reason to punish him further? Had she not had been so pretty and had he not had been drinking all night, at her expense, he probably, possibly wouldn't have, maybe even not said a word! However, he did and had and was now paying the price for it. With karma comes wisdom, he thought and he could certainly have done with some wisdom that fateful night.

The council had moved swiftly to belittle her story when it was printed in some of the daily papers. It was immediately panned by all the press that the council controlled which was most of them. Those few independent papers that did put some credence to her story were considered too flamboyant and out of touch with reality anyway that no one but the diehard conspiracy believers considered it worth reading. So it was eventually buried under the mundane news of the 'real' world. The reporter, Asil, had been sacked by her newspaper a little later for some silly reason but mainly because of the council applying more than a little pressure to the papers owners about their future publishing rights. She had tried to contact Ha'an again but he had avoided all contact with her and made it very clear that he never wanted to see her again. His life had already been ruined so why make it any worse. For he was now permanently based at Topside as he was considered a 'valuable asset' to the Smarian army. It also meant that the press couldn't get to him nor he to the press.

At midday, they stopped for a rest and to contact base. Dez very gingerly connected up the rear of the scorse to the tiny generator that powered the radio. He then moved around to the front of the scorse and, praying that he had connected everything up correctly, began to feed the scorse who he had named Woc. People don't normally name scorses but as Dez was spending most of his time with this scorse and had begun talking to it, he thought it only right that he should give it a name. After all, it never argued with him and always seemed to listen to what he said regardless of what he was saying. Something that Dez really wasn't used to. He even found himself patting Woc on the head affectionately as they walked behind the others. A friendship of sorts had been struck between a Smarian and a scorse.

Within a few moments, the food had worked and the scorse was doing exactly what it did naturally and the radio burst into life. Ha'an tuned the radio in and told base exactly where they were, which was interesting as he had never been the best, or even a mediocre, navigator in the Smarian army, and a vague guess as to their ETA at the rendezvous with Tega. A very vague guess as Ha'an didn't really know how long it would take or to be honest, really where they were. The radio operator at the base had acknowledged their position and advised him that there was a massive storm coming their way and that they should look for some shelter to ride it out.

Shelter, indeed, thought Ha'an, *the boy had obviously never been outside the base or he wouldn't have suggested such a ludicrous thing. Shelter out on Topside, indeed. It didn't exist!*

Ha'an gathered everyone together, except for Dez and his scorse, for obvious reasons as it was still munching away and farting, and explained the situation. They would push on towards the mountains until the storm was upon them. Hopefully, they could make it and see out the storm from one of the many caves that honeycombed the mountains. If not, they would have to ride it out in their tents and pray that they survived. What he didn't tell them was of the stories about the caves. How many, who had taken shelter in them, had told stories of ghostly lights and figures and the strange voices that tried to speak to them in their ancient tongue? So persistent were the voices that some were pushed to the point where they had opted to take their chances in their tents outside rather than stay in there a minute longer. Ha'an himself had previously seen these lights and heard the voices and he, too, had decided it better to stay outside rather than be taunted by them. But now, he had other people to consider and if the storm was as bad as he was informed, he would have to suffer the caves and all that might be in them. They got back in line and made for the mountains.

Soon the wind was getting up and the red dust had started its dance. Gently at first, as it started to swirl around their feet like water in a stream. Then, as the wind started to come in stronger from one direction, the red dust blew across their feet like waves on a beach. Gentle waves at first that soon began to get higher and higher until they were hitting them like waves hitting a breaker. Hitting them with such force that it was becoming a struggle to stay on their feet. Soon, all around them was awash with the red dust. They pushed on towards the mountains and their only hope of survival. The wind whipping up the dust in a frenzy now and making their path unclear. Tripping over the rocks that were now hidden by the swirling sand. Their vision was becoming very impaired even with their goggles on and Ha'an had advised them all to tie on to each other and to keep moving. His words were being lost in the ferociousness of the wind but he was able to make himself understood as one by one they tied themselves together in a line. He knew that these new recruits wouldn't survive out in the open so he was desperate to get them to the mountains and the dubious safety of its caves, at all costs. With each step, the wind was pushing them in all directions. As if alive, the wind would constantly change direction, making it harder and harder to keep going. Picking up rocks and throwing them into their path. Sapping the life from them so that they might be sacrificed to the wastelands and be as dead as their surroundings. The dust was everywhere. It blasted away at their bodies and made it hard for them to breath. Its awesome power made every step, a test of strength and character. To give up now would be to give up on life itself. Ha'an, through the dust storm, could barely make out the darkness of the mountains as they pushed on towards them.

Must keep going, he thought to himself as he pushed on towards what he hoped would be safety.

The wind was lashing the side of the mountains. Eating at their very flesh and slowly wearing the mountains down with its power. It may take centuries, but eventually the wind would win and the mountains would fall. But not today. Today the mountains stood tall and offered a safe haven for our brave party. They pushed on through this unyielding storm and eventually arrived at the foot of the mountains. With a sense of hope filling his body and with renewed strength, Ha'an moved around the mountain, feeling his way around, gripping on to the side as the wind tried desperately to pull him from its safety and into oblivion. For what seemed like an age, they clambered around the mountain. Ha'an's body, being pressed to the mountain side by the wind one second and then being torn away from it the next until finally he found a cave and shelter from the storm. They pushed on into the cave's depths until the wind was just a roaring noise behind them. Feeling their way with their hands as their goggles were still covered with the red dust, they collapsed there with exhaustion. Oblivious to their surroundings, they lay there for a moment to regain some of their strength and their senses that the wind had tried so hard to crush. The silence between them was broken a loud scream.

"NO! NO! Ha'an! Sergeant Ha'an!"

Ha'an got up as quickly as he could. Gathering his senses and wiping the dust away from his goggles, he moved to the end of the line where he found Krun. He was holding the thrayed remains of the rope. The other end had been attached to Dez and the scorse. Ha'an ran to the opening of the cave, closely followed by Krun, hoping upon hope to find them there but no...all he could see was the wall of red dust swirling around outside. Ha'an fell to his knees.

"I'll go out there and find him. He can't be far," cried Krun as he went to run past Ha'an out into the storm. He was held back by the tree-like arms of Athan. Krun tried to struggle but had no hope of escaping Athan's immense grip.

"He's gone," whispered Athan in his deep gentle voice. "He's gone!"

The next morning, the storm had dissipated and they came out of their cave. All were quiet. Fortunately they hadn't been visited by the ghosts of the caves but had only slept because of their exhaustion. Not even bothering to light a fire they had hardly spoken to one another that night. Still shocked by the loss of one of their ragtag team. Only glad that they had made it to the relative safety of the caves. Haunted by previous events.

Ha'an looked out over the landscape. Despite the storm raging all night, the landscape remained much the same. Now just calm and coldly quiet. The daylight now casting eerie shadows all around the wasteland like strange creatures waiting to catch them out again. What to do now? Should they carry on towards their rendezvous with Tega as were their orders or should they look for Dez and the scorse? Ha'an knew that the chances of Dez and the scorse surviving were next to none but the cold reality was that without the scorse, they had lost their vital power source needed to power the lamps and the means of communication. What to do, what to do?

Chapter 5

The Poet and the Reporter

The Herald, Biz to his friends to which there weren't too many, had a spring in his step that evening. He could hardly believe it when that nice young lady from that paper 'The Daily…' whatever it was, had phoned and asked to speak to him about publishing some of his poems. No one had ever shown an interest in his poems before. In fact, not many people actually knew that he wrote any poetry at all. His wife had always poured scorn on his 'waste of time hobby' and had never even tried to read or listen to any of it.

"Pure waste of time, if you ask me," she would have said. Not that he ever did ask her, as he already knew exactly what she'd say and he was right!

"Who reads poetry these days? No one! All poets are dreamers and waste their time sitting around all day whilst decent people are out working hard to try and make something of themselves. Who ever heard of a poet entering the Great Council? No one, that's who! They witter on about nothing important and expect people to pay to listen and read it! Wasteful!" and she would go on and on and on. By this time, Biz would have left the room and found a dark corner somewhere to try and gather some self-confidence to carry on.

No use arguing with someone who had already closed their mind to any possibilities of his work being of any worth.

But not today! Today he was going to meet someone who actually wanted to read his work! What joy!

He had jumped onto a bus just outside the Great Chambers as it was a bit too far to walk. No one made eye contact with anyone as usual as he sat next to an older woman. She had begrudgingly grunted as she moved over ever so slightly as to allow the Herald to sit down next to her on this crowded bus. It was full of the usual commuters and school kids. Their working and learning day over. All now making their way back to whence they came. The school kids were making all the noise as they talked amongst themselves at a volume so loud that all could hear regardless of whether they wanted to or not. They chatted not about what wonders they had learnt that day but about the more important things such as who was dating who and the latest boy or girl band that was the most popular that week. The knowledge imparted that day ever so eloquently by their teachers was now secreted to the back of their minds as unimportant data for another day. The rest of the bus just sat either looking aimlessly out of the window or tried to read their newspapers and books amidst the noise all around them. They were leaving the grand open avenues of the Grand Cavern where the many offices of the Great Council adorned the pavements. Monuments of the Great Ones, old and past, stood on plinths at the side of the avenues to perpetuate their assumed greatness lit by the finest and brightest of streetlights. Ornately decorated to suit their surroundings. The grand houses of the rich and famous were here. Their high fences and huge gated entrances guarding their privacy. Doing their best to keep the secret that they were as Smarian as the poorest of society. They, too, had feelings and their personal highs and lows, mainly the same. Only their wealth made them different, but who was to say that merely material goods made them happy? Sometimes, the poorest of Smarians, who were surrounded by loving friends and family, were the richest amongst them.

The bus travelled slowly past all the large department stores, where the rich and privileged shopped. The wives and girlfriends of politicians, merchants and celebrities all did lunch in their finery with their social climbing friends. Some were the most beautiful looking of Smarians on the outside whilst being the ugliest of society on the inside. Happily gutter snipping, all of those that didn't fit in at that moment in time. Next week, it could and would be someone else in their circle that was ridiculed. Such was how it went. Friendship would have no meaning here among those who sought to climb the social ladder of false acceptance at the expense of any who got in their way. Where the prices of the goods they bought and the meals they devoured were to impress those of the same mind-set. Bought to fit in whether liked or not and generally at extortionate prices, more than most Smarians' weekly wages. The bus continued its journey past here as they entered the middle-class part of Below. The houses and the streets, smaller but still detached from each other. The shops and restaurants, all artisan and slightly pretentious. Streetlights still glowed all day to allow all to see. Perfect for its local clientele. Onwards went the bus as more and more people got off at various stops along the way to be replaced by the less fortunate in society. Those that could only work in these areas but never afford to live there or fit in. Now they were getting to the more somewhat sleazy district of

Chingstow. Here the houses and the shops mingled together. All small and tightly bound as one. Streetlights were less and less if they worked at all. No one spoke to anyone unless they were well-known to them. Smarians walked with their gaze fixed to the floor in front of them for fear of anyone catching their eye and asking them something. To ask them a question or worse still, try to strike up a conversation! Unsavoury characters hanging around the street corners looking for what, only they knew.

The Herald got off the bus where he had been told to and made his way down the narrow, badly lit lane towards the meeting place. Caught up in his thoughts of fame, he ignored the dubious surroundings and characters that were watching him make his way to the small dingy bar at the end of the lane. There he thought he'd meet the person who was going to change his life and make all his dreams come true. Little did he know just how much an influence on his life this person was going to be but not in the way that he thought! He was so lost in his own little world that he never once thought that there was any ulterior motive to this reporter wanting to talk to him. Not once did he consider anything other than his own expectations of this meeting. Why should he? After all, he was merely the Herald to the 'Great One' and had knowledge of all manner of secrets that the Great Council didn't want the Smarian people to know about. Something that he never really thought too much about as most of the time no one wanted to listen to him anyway! He considered himself just the messenger and hadn't considered what exactly the messages were and how important they might be. Unfortunately for him, others had!

Asil was sitting in a corner of the bar with her back to the wall away from prying eyes and ears. She sipped her cocktail keeping her eyes fixed firmly on the door. She had dressed provocatively on purpose this time to distract anyone from her real intentions. The little black figure-hugging dress with the plunging neckline had worked its magic before. Her pale grey skin, jet black eyes and bright red lips had mesmerised many an unsuspecting soul. Her long dark purple hair immaculately crowning her head. Asil always looked after her hair as it was only females that had hair on their heads. All males were completely bald! She was a very pretty female and had used her beauty to get on in the world of newspapers. She played on the weaknesses of the Smarian males when it came to a pretty face. Often using it to get a story or wangle information out of some unwitting male to further her career, no matter what the consequences to the poor soul that she had deceived. Tonight would be no exception. Her prey wouldn't stand a chance. She sat contemplating what kind of information she may get out of the Herald. How easy it had been to get him to agree to meet her on the pretence of printing his poems. Just how gullible could he be? She wouldn't have to wait too long to find out.

The bar wasn't the nicest of places but she knew that this was the place to meet people that you didn't want others to know about. A place for clandestine meetings for all manner of people. From husbands cheating on wives and wives cheating on husbands to the more sinister of characters, wheeling and dealing in things that most descent people didn't even know or want to know about. Its array of tiny secluded booths clinging to the walls around the bar, with just a few tables and chairs in the middle, made it the perfect place to hold those very private meetings. What passed as a carpet bore the scars of disgruntled arguments. Stained with the aftermath of thrown drinks with the occasional blood stains from the more confrontational disagreements. The walls and ceiling were either brown or dark red. The poor lighting making it hard to tell. A small three-piece band of old musicians with an equally old singer who bore the scars of never making the big time but still with misplaced hope, playing the blues quietly in the corner. The bar itself was festooned with drunks telling anyone who would listen, and those who didn't care, how the world had done them wrong. How it wasn't their fault that they were where they were. It was always someone else's fault, never their own. The truth that they sought was somehow always at the bottom of the next glass. Wasting what little money they had on more booze, rather than spending it on finding a way to get out of their pointless world. Sinking further and further into the abyss. Surrounding themselves with the negativity of others sharing that same world and slipping further down the slippery slope to self-destruction. They all had grand ideas about what they would do to change things for the better but lacked the inclination to do it! What with these sad individuals, its poor lighting and even poorer décor, the place was well suited to its name, 'The Last Resort'. A reporter's paradise!

Would he turn up? Did he fall for her story about the poems? Are there others in this bar having clandestine meetings? Sure enough there were some shady characters sitting alone in the surrounding booths all nursing their drinks whilst watching all around. The occasional 'couple' that sat with eyes for only each other whilst at the same time watching to see if anyone else was watching them. Always looking to the door every time it opened hoping not to see anyone they knew. *Perhaps they were watching her? Perhaps the Herald had tumbled her and sent the Information Bureau to spy on her? Perhaps...* Her thoughts were interrupted by the opening of the entrance door and in walked the Herald. He looked around the bar like a boy looking for his dad in a place where neither the boy nor his father should be. Everyone had stopped and was looking at the Herald. You could hear a pin drop. He really did look out of place in such a den of inequity. The Herald was just about to turn and run when Asil caught his eye. He was so relieved to see a friendly face that he almost ran over to her. Distraction over, the bar descended slowly back about its murky business of mutterings and meetings.

"So glad you could make it," started Asil as the Herald hurriedly sat down next to her as closely as he could, more for safety than anything else. Looking nervously around the bar he was wondering why on earth someone as lovely as her even knew such a place existed.

Asil moved slightly away feeling uncomfortable about being so close to someone she was trying to deceive.

"Would you like something to drink? A beer perhaps?"

Biz nervously nodded his acceptance and Asil beckoned to the bartender to bring a beer over. He acknowledged her with a nod and started to pour the beer.

"Well," she said as Biz looked nervously around trying not to make eye contact with anyone but failing miserably. Fortunately for him, everyone else was trying to stay out of eye contact too, for fear of being found out.

"Did you bring me some of your work for me to read?" she enquired.

Biz just looked at her for a moment. Hearing the words but not comprehending what they meant.

"Your poems? Did you bring them?"

It took another second before he realised what she had said and that she was actually talking to him.

"Yes," he blurted out, "yes, I have them here," and he produced an array of papers all containing some kind of poem or another from out of his briefcase. Presenting them on the table in front of her in the same mess that he had taken them out, he continued to survey the bar nervously. This was not the kind of place that he had ever frequented and he was definitely letting it show.

"Oh," she said calmly looking at the pile of scribbled notes that the Herald thought worthy. "Anything in there that I shouldn't see?" Asil was staring directly at his briefcase.

"What?" inquired Biz breaking his wide-eyed stare of all and sundry.

"Your briefcase. The crest on it. Isn't it the one that you use to carry all those important documents for the Great One in?"

Biz still looked puzzled, as Asil continued.

"Not that I'm at all interested in that kind of thing. No, I'm purely a dreamer. A lost cause to the poets of this world," she said lying through her teeth and trying not to show her obvious curiosity as to what was truly inside the briefcase.

Biz looked down at his briefcase and the large crest of the Great Council that adorned it and realised what she had meant. He looked back at her and smiled nervously.

Phew, he thought. *If only she knew what documents were in there; the latest information on the object from the sky. The*

report from the base on Topside about it. The test results that
stated that the object with the markings on brought back by
Tega was in no language known on Smar and was certainly
not made from any substance found on this world. If only she
knew.

Unfortunately for him she did know!

"Ah, your beer." She gestured to the bartender to put it down next to Biz. She gave him the money and the bartender grunted something incoherent about the lack of tip and moved away counting it whilst cursing her.

"Now, let's see what we have here," she said looking at the mound of paperwork as Biz made a move for his beer. Quite accidentally on purpose, Asil managed to knock over Biz's beer straight into his lap as she was supposedly reaching for his poems. Biz leapt up quickly, screaming, as the cold beer hit his lap and soaked his trousers. Asil, appearing innocent of the crime, quickly took out her handkerchief and tried to mop up the spilt beer down Biz trousers whilst attempting to apologise with every word. This just made things worse for Biz as he was not used to beautiful women mopping down the front of his trousers. Come to think of it, he wasn't used to any woman touching his nether regions! After all, he was married! Embarrassed and shocked, he stood there not knowing quite what to do but wishing that he would do something. Should he stop her from mopping his nether regions with her handkerchief as it really didn't look too good or should he allow her to continue because, after all, she was only trying to help?

The bar had now turned its attention towards them as Biz was standing up making an incoherent noise whilst Asil continued to mop him down whilst saying how sorry she was for doing this to him. Everyone in the bar were now making their own assumptions as to what was happening when Asil suggested that he go to the rest room to tidy himself up. Biz agreed quickly and made his way across the bar to the restroom, still making incoherent noises and muttering to himself whilst rubbing his crutch making it look worse as he went.

Asil waited until he was out of sight before grabbing his briefcase. Surprised that it wasn't locked, she quickly scanned the papers for something that she thought she could use. The speed at which she did this confirming that this was definitely something that she had done before. Euricka! She hadn't bargained on finding something quite like this. She read faster to see what more there was. The report from the base, their findings, the team being sent out! This was certainly worth the subterfuge. She quickly folded the papers into her own bag and used some of the Herald's own poems to replace what she took. That done, she placed the briefcase back where it was and sat back. A large grin had crept across her face but she had to control herself. He would be back from the restroom soon and she couldn't afford for him to become suspicious. No, she must be cool and play out this little scenario and get shot of him as quickly as possible.

Biz emerged from the restroom looking worse than he went in. The damp patch had now expanded to most of his trousers making a complete mess.

"I, er, I think I should leave now," he said looking down at his trousers and back at Asil hoping that she could magically dry him off and turn the clock back. What had started for him as a wonderful evening had quickly turned into a disaster.

"Yes, of course," replied Asil trying to hide the fact that she too couldn't wait to get out of there and back to her office to really read through the documents and see exactly what she had got.

"Perhaps we can meet up another time to discuss your poems?" she enquired trying to keep up the facade.

"Yes, yes," replied Biz as he picked up his briefcase and used it as a shield to hide his embarrassing damp patch. "Yes, another time," he said as he raced for the door forgetting all about his poems and his great expectations of the day. Now all he wanted to do was escape this place.

"Yes, another time," said Asil to herself as she watched him run through the doors. "Another time, indeed!"

With the Herald now through the doors and well on his way, Asil got up and with a broad smile on her face moved towards the door. Feeling extremely pleased with herself that her plan had been a success and that she had got more than she could have dreamed, she couldn't wait to tell her boss all about it. Show him the papers that would vindicate her. To prove to the world that she was right about the falling objects and that the Great Council knew all about it but covered it up. Yes, they will pay for making her look an idiot. She would publish the documents and see what the Great Council had to say about it. She didn't once think about the trouble that she would get the Herald into, not that she was bothered about it anyway.

Stupid man should have been more careful, she thought to herself as she made her way past the dodgy characters inside the bar. So wrapped up in her own success was she, that she didn't notice one of the customers slowly putting down and neatly folding his newspaper as she passed and watching intently as she left. Slowly rising out of his chair and quite purposefully following her out and down the road, newspaper under his arm.

Chapter 6

Alive!

"Oh, yes! How delightful. Yes, do it some more…" Dez awoke with a start and a large wet tongue slapping around his face. The fact that he could awaken at all missed him at first. He was too busy wiping the slobber from his face deposited by an overzealous Woc to think about the night before. Then very quickly, last night events started to run through his head and they filled him with dread. The storm! A cold shiver shot down his spine. He remembered the rope holding him to Krun coming undone and his frantic efforts to call them being lost in the howling wind. He remembered trying desperately to keep up. Shouting at them, hoping upon hope that they might hear him. His words being torn from his mouth and despatched to the four corners of the desert by that devil of a wind. It was as if the storm was saying, "Not today! Today you are mine and mine alone!" How he had eventually lost sight of them amidst the ravages of the storm. How he had tried to push on alone, to try and find them but finally succumbing to pure exhaustion and the power of the storm. Laying down in the sand, defeated for what he thought was his last moments. Remembering this a little too well he slumped back on the sand again, a deflated Smarian.

A cold wet tongue slapped him in the face again. Wiping his face with disgust, he looked up at Woc who seemed genuinely pleased to see him. Well, he was actually guessing that Woc was pleased to see him as there is very little expression on a scorse's face at the best of times. Looking around at the now quiet landscape, Dez began to wonder where he was and how he survived the night in the middle of a storm. Slowly it was coming back to him and Dez began to realise what had happened. He remembered falling to the ground with exhaustion and giving up. He remembered how Woc had wrapped himself around him and wondering why but being too tired to care. Now he understood! Woc had done it to protect him and itself from the storm. *Of course*, he thought, *these creatures survived out here in the wastelands long before the Smarians had domesticated them.* Perhaps the long chats with Woc or more likely the fact that Dez fed him must have formed some kind of bond between them. Either way, they were alive! Dez started to stand up and Woc quickly uncoiled himself and stood beside him.

"I'm alive!" he shouted at the top of his voice, looking to the sky with his arms raised in defiance. "YE-HA!" he continued and started to do a little dance. It was about then that he had a little reality check and stopped dead in mid-dance. Yes, he was indeed alive. Yes, they had survived the storm but where the hell were they? Dez looked straight at Woc.

"Don't suppose you know, do you?"

Dez wasn't sure if he was expecting an answer or not but when one didn't come, he just thought, *no, I didn't think so.*

He looked around and surveyed his position. There was no sign of the others, just the desert in every direction. He could see some mountains in the distance, but were they the ones that they were heading for last night? He had no way of knowing as he may have wandered around in any direction last night during the storm, before he collapsed.

Well, this is a bit of a dilemma, he thought quite calmly for some strange reason. Perhaps, the truth of his 'dilemma' hadn't really hit him yet. Perhaps, he was still suffering from the shock of awakening on his own in the middle of nowhere! He thought for a while. Looking around hopefully for the slightest chance that he may see one of the others or anyone else, really! He wasn't fussed about who they were or what they were doing there, just so long as they had some idea of how to get out of this godforsaken place. With not too many other options open to him and no one else turning up, he eventually decided that his best chance was to head towards the mountains, whether they were the right ones or not.

What's the worst that could happen? he thought and with that, he picked up the end of Woc's lead and off he headed towards the mountains with his faithful scorse, Woc, following on behind. In hindsight, he really probably shouldn't have thought, what's the worst that could happen, as with his run of bad luck the 'worst' probably would!

Still weary from the previous night and his mind still full of the 'what ifs' following what could have been tragic events, Dez wandered across the wasteland in a dazed trance-like state towards the mountains. Unfortunately, as he wasn't paying much attention to his surroundings, not something he did much better when he was in his normal mental state of mind either really, he hadn't been fully aware that his feet were slowly getting deeper and deeper into the sand. This didn't bother Woc as having so many legs, its weight was so well dispersed that it didn't sink into the sand. More floated over the top of it rather like a big stick in a stream. It wasn't until he was almost up to his knees and struggling to move that Dez finally began to realise that something might be a tad wrong. Looking down and seeing that his feet had disappeared into the sand up to his knees, Dez realised what he had stupidly and unwittingly done. He had wandered into one of the many quick sandpits! The more he struggled to get out, the deeper he got into the sand. Woc had now begun running around in circles, being of no help whatsoever whilst Dez was slowly being sucked into the ground.

Typical, thought Dez. *Just as I thought luck was on my side, I wander into this. Could have died in my sleep and not known anything about it but nooo…I had to survive that and suffer a worse fate. I sometimes wonder why I bother,* thought Dez with an air of reluctant acceptance of his current predicament.

"What else can go wrong today?"

He was about to find out as just at that point two bright lights appeared hovering above the sand. As Dez had already resigned himself to dying in the quicksand, he decided to stop struggling and observe the bright lights, for he had no idea what they were or why they had suddenly appeared. After all, he wasn't going anywhere but down! Were they a sign that he was about to enter the after-world? Guardians of the gateway there to lead him to a better place, perhaps? Something that his barmy old grandmother had often wittered on about but he never bothered listening to.

Too young for all that, he had thought, *I'll wait until it happens!*

Well, perhaps now was his chance as it looked like it might just be happening!

"Should we help him?" Enquired one of the lights. Its brightness flickered with every word as it spoke.

Well, Dez wasn't sure if it had actually spoken or not, as it seemed to be more in his head than someone speaking directly to him.

"Don't think we're allowed to," replied the other. "Something about timelines being altered and all manner of things changing if we did, they had warned in class. Remember?"

Dez banged his head with his right hand to see if that would make the sounds come out of his head…or go away. He wasn't fussed which.

"Yes, I know but it does seem a bit harsh. I mean, he's just one Smarian alone out here. What harm could it do?" queried the other, completely ignoring Dez's presence.

Nope! It hadn't worked. It was still as if the conversation between them was going on inside his head. He relaxed a bit and thought he'd see where the conversation went. After all, he still wasn't going anywhere and perhaps he was just going mad! Either way, it might be entertaining. Better than dying alone, if in fact he was alone! Who knew?

"Oh, it could change the past in ways that could bring the fall of Smar as we know it," continued one of the lights. Dez had lost track of which was which and didn't much care by now anyway.

"After all, he could be the one that stops them making contact with those from the blue planet and then we might never be. Oh no, we can't mess with the timelines."

Having heard enough of himself being talked about in the third person, Dez decided it was time he said something. What harm could it do to interact with these voices as they may well be just in his head anyway, he wondered.

"OI!" piped up Dez. "I don't care much about timelines. Give me a hand!"

"Give me a hand!" chortled one. "We don't have hands. Haven't had them for centuries. Pure energy, you know. Much more civilised."

"Civilised," retorted Dez. "You're floating there watching me sink into the sand and you call yourself civilised! Doesn't seem very civilised to me!"

"Well, of course, we are. You're just far too primitive to comprehend it. I mean, we're just visiting here for a history exam. Thought we might benefit from seeing what it was really like when we stumbled across you. To be honest, we're not supposed to interact but when we saw your predicament, we couldn't see the harm. Not like you're going to tell anyone is it!" and with that they both started laughing out loud, much to Dez's annoyance.

"Perhaps you could answer some questions?" inquired the other one.

"Answer some questions! Don't you think I've got better things to do with what's left of my time than answer your silly questions? It may have escaped your notice but I'm a bit busy dying at the moment!" cried Dez in desperation for them to do something.

"Well, if you're just going to be rude, we'll leave you to it. Honestly, whatever happened to manners in this century?" and with, that they started to fade away.

"This century? Where are you muppets from? What other century is there?" shouted Dez in an attempt to keep them there. At least he could have a conversation with something before he died.

Woc was still running around in circles, creating clouds of dust everywhere and was still being of no use to Dez at all.

They stopped fading away and began to shine again. This raised Dez's hopes that they might actually help him. However they just continued to talk at him.

"Oh, there are multiple centuries in multiple universes at any given time. Each one slightly different than the other. Have you never wondered what it would be like if you made a different decision somewhere along the line? What would have happened if you went left instead of right, studied harder or less? Perhaps not less in your case! Well, somewhere in a parallel universe the consequences of every decision you have or haven't made are played out. Like what would have happened if you hadn't been pushed to the front to take this mission? Where would you be now if you had paid attention at basic training and learnt how to tie a knot properly? What if your parents hadn't met? You wouldn't have been born and some other poor fellow might have been put in your position. The possibilities are endless. Each universe occupying the same place and point in time. Each oblivious of each other. In some, you are a hero whilst in others you are the villain. In this one for instance, you are…well, you just are! We, on the other hand, know all about these universes and are able to transverse them at will. Time and space have no barriers for us. We can go backwards or forwards in time and space. Even sideways, if we want! We look at the likes of you as merely microbes under the microscope assuming you know what a microscope is! Gives one a much more rounded view of things. Now about these questions…"

Dez was now completely lost as to what the light was saying. He had a hard-enough time getting up in the morning, let alone transverse time and space! All he wanted in this time and in this space was to get out of the damn quicksand!

"We must go now!" said the other light with an urgency.

"Why? It was just getting interesting. I'm sure I could convince him to tell us more if only…oh, I see!" and with that they both disappeared in an instant.

Well, that's just rude, thought Dez, *leaving in such a hurry without asking for leave or anything! Could have held on until I'd gone under, at least! Funny things, though. I wonder what they meant by microbes under a…what did they call it? A microscope?*

Just as this and many other thoughts were going through Dez's small and somewhat bewildered mind, he realised that he was now up to his neck in the sand. Woc was nowhere to be seen. Not that he could see a lot from where he was anyway, apart from all the dust that Woc had stirred up. He pondered over what was going to happen next. Is there life after death? Will he descend or ascend to a better life beyond Topside? Will it hurt?

Fortunately for him, he didn't get the chance to find out for just as his head went under and all around started to go dark, he felt a sharp tug at his neck. Someone or something was pulling him out from the sand. Slowly at first and then with more urgency, he found himself being released from the deadly grip of the quicksand.

What now? he thought as he was being dragged upwards and along. *Surely I've suffered enough. I was just getting used to the idea of suffocating. Now what? Probably some kind of animal that wants me for a meal! From one miserable way of dying to another. What was best? Suffocating under the sand or being torn apart by a vicious animal?*

He continued to think these most awkward of questions as he slowly popped out from the sand like a cork from a bottle. He never did get his answer for as it turned out it was neither. As he was being pulled along the sand to what he thought was a certain horrible death, he could swear that he could hear the voices again.

Those really nice lights have pulled me free, at last, he thought quickly redressing all the bad things that he had said about them.

"Dez!" said a voice as again Dez thought he was back under the sand again but this time it was just Athan's enormous chest that was suffocating him.

"Let him breath!" shouted another voice.

Athan released his grip and dropped Dez to the floor. He took a much-needed big breath and opened his eyes and looked straight up at the faces of his comrades. He looked at Ha'an, then Krun, Karel and then Athan. All were smiling with joy and started to laugh.

"We thought we'd lost you!" exclaimed Krun. "When I realised that you weren't with us in the cave, I was beside myself with grief. Unusual for me. For a moment, I couldn't see the bright side. Did in the end though. You not being there made for more room in the cave, etc…I never thought that I would see you again."

Krun's habit of always finding a positive side of thinking could sometimes be really annoying! Especially when you had almost died!

Ha'an was now trying to catch the scorse, who thought it was a good game to run as soon as Ha'an came anywhere near the lead. Timing it just right to give Ha'an a chance to get it and then running off a short distance until he tried again. Ha'an was using some colourful language and gestures though no one could, fortunately, make out exactly what he was saying.

"Well, just how did you find me?" asked Dez sitting up and brushing the sand off from all over himself.

"It was the scorse," explained Karel. "We saw a dust cloud and came to see what it was. I thought it was a natural phenomenon and asked Ha'an about it, whether he'd seen anything like it before. Should we go and look at it or just ignore it? Was it something being created by whatever it was that landed here? Ha'an didn't answer me. He just started screaming something and running in this direction away for me. Turns out it was just that stupid scorse running around in circles that had created the dust cloud whilst you were sinking to your death. Luckily for you, we saw it."

"Luck? No, that wasn't luck. That was a very clever scorse saving my life!"

Dez took off his boots and let the sand escape as he went on to explain about the way Woc, yes, that was what he called it, had kept him safe during the storm by coiling up around him and about the lights that taunted him whilst he sank into the sand. He couldn't really tell them much about what the lights had said as most of it had been well above his intelligence level! Anyone know what a micro something was? They all looked a bit confused and sceptical about what Dez was saying and put it down to being alone out there during the storm. Yes, the scorse could have curled up and saved his life but talking lights in the sky from somewhere not Smar? That they drew the line at.

"I can believe what you say about the scorse as it has been known before for a scorse to bond with a Smarian." explained Ha'an as he had now caught the scorse and was listening to Dez's story. "As for the lights. Well, best you keep that to yourself."

Dez wanted to try and make them believe him about the lights but began to wonder if, in fact, it had happened at all. Had it all been in his head after all? He definitely recalled it sounding like it was just in his head but he didn't recall it being there before! Confusing himself, he decided not to dwell on it any more as it was beginning to give him headache!

All dusted off and ready to go, Ha'an spoke to them.

"Well, we're a bit behind now so let's crack on and try and make up to time. We're still a long way from our rendezvous with Tega."

With pats on the back for everyone and the team now together again, they moved onwards across the wastelands to whatever lay ahead. Dez still brought up the rear along with his newfound friend. Nothing was going to separate him and his mate, Woc. The scorse that had saved his life.

Ha'an, happy that they had found Dez and the scorse, led them towards the mountains again knowing that they must go through the shortcut that Tega had marked on the map. What he didn't do was tell the others what had happened the last time he used that route. The time when he and a few other had been sent to see what had landed previously. How he was the only one to survive! That he kept to himself!

Chapter 7
The First Landing

It's going to be a Strange day! Ha'an thought as he listened to Captain Abisp lay out his plan of attach. He had been perfectly happy finishing his national service on Topside before all this happened. Eleven months and fifteen days of keeping his head down, saying "Yes sir, no sir" like any other good recruit just wanting to get back to normal life at Below. But no. No, something had to land on Smar and he had been one of the chosen 'lucky' few to go and see what it was. Well that's how the commandant had described this 'Wonderful opportunity' to them anyway. Not that they had any choice in the matter!

"To capture it if they could for scientific study" had been the other thing the commandant had said.

Ha'an had thought that if the scientists had wanted it that badly then perhaps they should have been the ones to go and get it! Wrong! Apparently the scientists were too valuable an asset to risk on such a dangerous venture. Hence, he and his compatriots were there!

"Well lads, that's what we'll do once we see this thing. Take command of the situation. Let it know who's the boss and take it back to where the scientists can study it. Easy!" proclaimed the captain.

Well, it certainly sounded easy. However, like all the best plans (And this certainly wasn't the best plan!), there was a slight problem. No one had ever tried to capture a machine that wasn't from Smar. A machine that just might not conform to the captain's well thought out plan. Something that they would have to find out, unfortunately for them, sooner rather than later!

A lookout came clambering over the hill running as fast as he could whilst shouting at the top of his voice, "It's coming, it's coming!" His comrade just behind him. He, too, screaming the same.

Captain Abisp, a short rather stout chap with a middleclass accent, looked as if he was about to explode with the enjoyment of his expected success. His chest pushed out and his shoulders back, he turned back to his men and shouted, "Right then! Let's get ready. You there! Get that rope pulled tight across its path. You lot, get ready to climb on board and make the blighter surrender!"

The recruits, including Ha'an, pulled hard on the rope stretching it across the path. A whining sound could be heard in the background and then it appeared as it came over the hill. It was huge. About three times the size of any house at Below. Silver in colour, its surface glistened in the sun as it slowly moved towards them without any fear. Six wheels that turned and gyrated as it made its way across the red dust of Topside. Stopping every now and then, for a brief moment, before moving on as if deciding on which direction to go. Avoiding the bigger rocks and making short work of the not so big ones as it crushed them beneath its huge metal wheels. It had a strange looking turret mounted high on several masts secured to the main body that swung around in different directions.

This, too, made weird whining noises as it spun around as if surveying its surroundings although it seemed to ignore the recruits as it approached. Two giant wing-like plates sprung out on both sides of this moving machine and reflected the sun's rays upwards. It really was a monster of a machine.

"Get ready!" shouted the captain from a safe distance to the side and away from the path of this machine.

"To get a better view of the operation." he had told them earlier explaining why he would be stationed there.

To get as far away in case anything goes wrong! thought everyone else! They were right, of course.

The recruits tensed as the machine approached the rope now blocking its path.

"Ready!" shouted captain Abisp, again.

All of them pulled even harder and braced for contact as the machine was almost upon them. Well, it didn't even slow down as it grabbed the rope with the sharp grips protruding from the wheels and deposited it in the dust, pulling all the recruits to the ground as it went. Carrying on forwards as if they weren't there, this machine moved past the troop dragging the rope and the recruits a short way before all of them let go and the rope lay useless on the ground. The trap sprung unsuccessfully as all, barred the captain and his two officers, now had their faces in the dust.

"Hmm!" pondered Abisp. "Playing hard to get, eh!"

Playing hard to get! It hadn't even seen them as it passed. Not once did it acknowledge their existence. It just kept going on its merry way. Moving this way and that, as it went around the rocks as if looking for something other than them.

Ha'an and the others slowly pulled themselves up from the ground and dusted themselves down. The captain called his two officers, who had also been standing clear of this machine, to his side. There they entered into a huddle and were now discussing their next 'Great' plan. Ha'an had watched the machine as it disappeared into the distance. Continuing on its aimless route. The two lookouts now following it as it went.

That night around the campfire, the two lookouts had returned and told of how the machine stopped soon after the sun went down. As if it too had made camp for the night. How the turret had stopped moving around and dropped slowly as if it slept. Once they had thought it safe to leave they marked where it was on the map and made it back to camp. No one had ever seen anything like this before. There were no known records of machines that roamed the surface ever being here before. Sure, there had been some strange things that had hit the surface in the past. Some had exploded as they hit, spreading rocks and debris everywhere. Creating huge dust clouds as it hit and scarring the landscape with a massive crater that would glorify the size of the object that hit. There were stories of some weird silver things that survived impact. Making very little dust fly up and no crater. How they had opened up like a flower, but then just sat there doing nothing. Eventually being covered up by the red dust stirred up by the storms. Covered up and forgotten about. Never before though had anything roamed the surface as this thing did. It, too, had landed making very little dust and certainly no crater. It had unfolded as before but unlike the previous objects, this one had started to move. It had escaped the cocoon that had surrounded it and made off into the desert. Hence, they were sent here to see what it was and what it was doing.

Captain Abisp and his two officers were sitting around another fire. For some reason, the captain thought that he and his officers were too important to sit with the recruits. Not only did they sit separately, they ate separately too. Associating with the recruits only when they had to.

"Better for discipline!" he had said.

Not that the recruits complained but it did create a bit of a 'them and us' syndrome.

The two officers were leaning forward and intently listening to what the captain had to say. Offering up opinions every now and then as deep in conversation they remained. Discussing something but they weren't letting on what it was.

That night, Ha'an lay awake thinking about that machine. How it didn't stop. How it had ignored them completely. How it just kept on going as they tried to get it to stop. What could they possibly do to stop this thing, let alone capture it? He fell asleep that night without any of his questions answered. All he was worried about was what farcical, haphazard plan the captain and his two officers would come up with next!

The next morning, the captain announced his new improved plan. A plan that wouldn't fail! As he explained what they, not him, were going to do, they all looked horrified. Even the two officers didn't look happy about it for they had to take part as well this time! Everyone listened hoping that the captain was going to finish with an, "Only joking!" but he wasn't and didn't. He carried on talking, being very visual as he explained how they would stop this infernal machine once and for all. Plan explained and with a "No time for questions!" in case anyone had a valid point to bring up, they packed up and marched to where the machine was last spotted. The recruits had been selected well as none of them had the confidence to say what they all felt or the audacity to question captain Abisp's orders. None would rebel against the captain's ludicrous idea. Even the cleric that had been "lucky" enough to be granted the chance to see this thing first-hand by the Great One didn't say a word. He had long since accepted his fate. They all just went along with it, trying not to think too hard about the possible negative consequences.

They had arrived at the spot where the lookouts had said that the machine had stopped only to find that it wasn't there anymore. A very brief moment of belief for the recruits before one of the lookouts, seeing that Abisp wasn't a very happy Smarian captain at the prospect of losing it, pointed out that they could easily follow the machine's enormous tracks. A smile appeared back on the captain's face as he gestured and mumbled something about them going on ahead whilst they followed. The faces of the recruits dropped again. Hope of a reprieve dashed, they despairingly followed the two lookouts as they tracked the machine.

It didn't take long before they could see the machine in the distance. It was doing its usual random dance of going in this way and that direction. Its high turret spinning around aimlessly as it went. Avoiding the larger rocks and crushing the smaller ones as it went over them much as before. Sometimes it would go right up to a boulder as if challenging it only to reverse and find another route around it. Over the many hills of Topside, it trundled away until it suddenly stopped!

Now's our chance, thought the captain as he shouted for everyone to get into position.

The recruits broke up into three groups. The officers each took eight recruits and headed off. One group went to the front and one went behind the machine. The other 'group' consisted of Ha'an and Fisah. They had been given the 'honour', as captain Abisp had put it, of jumping on the machine and disabling it. Just how they were supposed to disable it was described to Ha'an and Fisah as a 'small stumbling point'. A stumbling point that they would 'have to use their initiative' to solve. For how on Smar was anyone supposed to know how to disable something that no one knew anything about! Ha'an and Fisah just looked at each other, shrugged their shoulders and did as they were told. Neither had any idea of what they were going to do when they got on top of the machine but both knew that there was no point in arguing about it.

The group that had gone to the back had tied two ropes to the huge backwheels of the machine. Securing each rope as best they could to a large rock. The group at the front had put as many rocks as they could underneath each of the equally large front wheels. They, too, had also tied a rope to each wheel and were standing ready to pull as hard as they could to finally capture this machine. Abisp was standing directly in front of the machine. His legs apart and all arms folded in, he stood proudly looking up at the machine in premature triumph. Whilst all this was going on, Ha'an and Fisah were climbing up one of the middle wheels to the machine's main body. It was easily three times their height and was wider than their outstretched arms could reach. As they climbed, they noticed that there was some form of large drill busily making a hole in the ground directly beneath the machine. Not wishing to get caught on the wheel if this thing decided to move, they didn't stop to study what it was doing, just continued up to the top. Fortunately, there were enough nooks and crannies on this monster to make the rest of the climb almost easy. They had both also noticed that four huge strange symbols were adorning the side of the machine that made no sense to Ha'an or Fisah as they climbed. Both too intent on reaching the top to spend any time studying either. Once at the top, they could see for miles all around Topside. An uninterrupted view of this barren wasteland. No time to admire the view, they surveyed the top of the machine. The masts that held the turret were higher than they had originally thought. Easily twice the height of the main body of the machine. The turret itself looked as if it had two massive eyes on either side of the revolving platform. Eyes that were busy looking over the horizon. Too high to have seen the troops below. The main body itself was relatively flat. Towards the back, there was a large what looked like an upside-down dome pointing upwards with a long spike in the centre. The two huge wing-like pieces were a golden colour on top. These shone brightly in the sun dazzling Ha'an and Fisah's eyes, causing them to look away. It was like being on a mobile parade ground set high above the ground with just the two of them standing there all alone. In order to see and hear the captain, they made for the front of the machine. Not standing too close to the edge, they peered over to see what was going on below. They could see Abisp looking all important and telling the front group to be ready. A faint voice from the back confirming that they, too, were in position and awaiting further orders.

Ha'an and Fisah carried on looking around the surface of the machine for any sign of a clue as to how to stop it. They decided to start at the front and work their way to the back. The top of the machine was made up of a multitude of panels, all tightly secured down. Some were smaller than others but each having more of those strange symbols on them. They could hear what they assumed as the drill burrowing on below them as they continued looking until all of a sudden the drill stopped. Another noise took over for a brief moment then nothing. The silence was deafening. They strained their ears to hear if anything else was going to happen. It wasn't a noise that startled them, more of a jolt as the machine tried to start moving again. They raced back to the front as they could hear Abisp shouting at the recruits to pull harder. The machines whining noise grew louder until it began ever so slowly to edge forward.

"Hold it back!" cried Abisp as he joined the recruits who were now wrapping the rope around themselves in an attempt to try and restrain this monster. The machine's whining grew louder. The group at the back now attaching themselves to the rope as did the front to try and pull harder and stop the beast. The rocks under the front wheels started to crumble as the machine tried hard to break free. Louder and louder got the whining until it just stopped. It took a moment for it to register with everyone and then they began to cheer. Abisp was laughing out loud, immediately thinking that his fantastic plan had worked. However, this was all too soon as without hesitation the machine began to reverse. No one had expected this! The recruits at the back were still tied tightly to the rope as the huge metal wheels moved over them. Crushing them like the small rocks earlier as the wheels turned and before they could untie and escape. Their screams of desperation filled the air. The group at the front desperately tried pulling the monster back. Straining on the ropes with all their might to try and save their fellow recruits. Success! The machine stopped again but it was too late for the group at the back. All had perished under the wheels of this unyielding monster. The remaining recruits at the front released their grip on the rope. Not a word was said as they slumped to the floor, still in the path of the machine. None were aware until it was too late that the machine had started its whining again and began to move forward. Forward over the exhausted fallen recruits still tied to its front wheels. Their cries were short lived as it moved slowly and unmercifully over them. The last voice being that of the captain as he had tried desperately to push it back. To try and save his recruits. To try and save himself! His last words of "Oh bother! That didn't work, did it?" blurted out in surrender as he, too, was crushed to a pulp quickly and with no mercy by this monstrous beast.

Ha'an and Fisah looked at each other in horror. Not only had they lost everyone in their troop, they were trapped on board the monster as it moved onwards. The bodies of their fallen comrades left in the dust as it made its way across Topside.

"What do we do now?" asked Fisah.

Ha'an thought for a moment. The cries of the recruits still fresh in his head. The words of the captain stating the obvious. What will they do? What can they do? He had no idea. Only the words of Abisp stuck in his head. "Use your initiative", not "Oh bother! That didn't work, did it?"

Nothing sprung to mind as Ha'an sat down. The motion of the machine moving forward was making it hard to stand even with his tail adding to his balance. Fisah joined him. Not a word passed between them for what seemed like an age.

Think! thought Ha'an, *think!*

And so they did. Ha'an had started to hit the machine in frustration. Harder and harder, he hit it until all of a sudden one of the panels sprung open. Fisah looked at Ha'an. Both surprised by what had happened. This impenetrable machine had just popped open! They both jumped up and after quickly looking at each other, began pulling hard on the open panel. Trying to peel it back to reveal what was inside. Not knowing what they might find. Was it a doorway leading to whatever was driving this machine? A trap to lure them in only to close shut behind them almost as quickly as it had opened? Who knew? They continued to pull until finally the panel flew off and deposited itself on the surface of the machine. Again, they looked at each other apprehensively and then into the hole where once the panel had been. They peered in wondering what to expect only to see an array of brightly coloured cables. Nothing more. No steps leading into the bowels of this monster. Just cables!

"What now?" asked Ha'an, scratching his head. He hadn't expected there to be just cables. Strange creatures or smaller metal machines that powered and drove this monstrous machine, but not just cables!

Fisah looked up at Ha'an, then back at the cables. Scratched his head too and looked back at Ha'an.

"Haven't got a clue!" he announced and sat down again. Ha'an did the same. Both surprised and now thinking about what to do next.

"Why don't we just cut through them and see what happens?" offered up Fisah.

Ha'an thought for a second. Neither had any idea what would happen. It might stop the machine or it might anger it. Either way, it was the only thing that they had thought of that they actually could do. The thought of travelling around on the back of this machine until it hopefully stopped that evening had occurred to them, but what if it didn't stop? What if it carried on all night further into the wilds of Topside? A storm might occur and they would be left helpless and open to the elements. This and a lot of other negative thoughts were running through their heads until they both decided to hack away at the cables and see what happened.

It wasn't easy. Their knives easily went through the colourful outer layer casing but they struggled to make any headway against the thick metal cable inside. Taking it in turns, they cut and hacked their way slowly through the first cable. They waited patiently for a reaction. Nothing! The machine just kept going. Well, that didn't work so they carried on and started to hack away at the next cable. It wasn't until they were halfway through the second cable that something happened. Whether it was them cutting their way through the cable or for some other reason, the machine lurched to one side. Almost turning itself on its side, landed in a gulley. Its wheels continued to turn this way and that. Gyrating around in every direction and backwards and forwards to no avail. Trying everything it could to release itself from the gulley it had fallen into. Ha'an and Fisah took their chance. They let go of the side of the hole that they had grabbed as the machine fell. Now sliding down the back of the machine towards the ground, jumping clear at the last moment to safety. As soon as they hit the ground, they ran as fast and as far away from that machine as they could. Only stopping once to see if it had worked its way free and was giving chase. It hadn't. The machine was still stuck in the gulley and making its whining noise as if frustrated by its predicament.

Once they were a far enough distance away from the machine, they sat on the floor and reflected over what had happened. Grieved for those poor recruits that had lost their lives to that monstrosity. Now they had to make it back to base and break the terrible news of what had happened.

It had taken them almost a week to get close to base. A week in which Fisah had confided in Ha'an that he didn't want to go back. Unlike Ha'an he still had another eight months to go and, after this missions events, didn't fancy his chances of survival. He had seen enough of Topside and its unusual events for a lifetime. They were coming close to the entrance to Below and Fisah had decided that he was going to try and sneak back in and head for the north and hide out there. Easy enough up there as it was sparsely populated. Ha'an had tried to talk him out of it but had eventually agreed to say that Fisah, too, had been crushed by the machine. No one need ever know the truth. They hugged before they parted. Fisah, to hopefully start a new life in the north whilst Ha'an headed back to the base. Now there was only Ha'an left to tell the story!

Chapter 8
Caves and What Lies Within

It was starting to get dark as they approached the entrance to the shortcut through the mountain. The huge entrance looked as if it had been carved out of the mountain, rather than formed naturally. Perfectly straight on both sides, with an arch at the top as if it had been done on purpose. Tapering back to the much smaller yet very square cave entrance. There seemed to be time-worn symbols or writing above the entrance as if to announce itself as the way through the mountain but they made no sense. They were all looking at the main entrance in awe at its size and reverence as they approached it. Not sure what to make of something so perfect in this land of harsh ruggedness and chaos that it looked well out of place. Nothing natural could have made this, could it? None of them had ever seen anything quite like it before except for Ha'an. He remembered it only too well. Ha'an felt an uneasy feeling of déjà vu as they wandered through the grand entrance to the cave. Memories of his last visit shot through his brain and sent him cold. Remembering the strange lights and voices that had made some of his compatriots run back out screaming into the night, never to be seen again. He walked in with every one of his senses working overtime. Wishing that there was another way but knowing that there wasn't. He kept in front for two reasons. One to show no fear for the sake of his subordinates behind him and two, so that they couldn't see the fear in his eyes!

As they made their way inside, the sheer size of the entrance made them feel quite insignificant and humble. They all looked around as they entered still in awe at the immense size of the entrance and the majesty of it. It seemed more like a gaping hole between one world to another rather than a shortcut through the mountain. The ground began to slope downwards as deeper into the entrance they went. Woc stopped and Dez had to tug really hard to get him to move. It seemed all of them were more than just a little apprehensive of going in as the mountain and the darkness began to swallow them up. Ha'an took out his lantern and lit it. The others did the same as they all moved further into the cave. No one talked or made a sound. Not even Karel had any questions! It was as if they didn't want to wake anything, if in fact there was anything in there to wake. The lanterns threw their light all around the enormous cave. Bouncing off the walls and allowing the shadows to dance across the cave with a great joy of being free at last from the darkness. Their dance short-lived but all the better for it as they celebrated their brief two-dimensional life before being imprisoned again. To wait for the light to appear once more and another chance to dance again.

Dez walked with one eye closed and held on very tightly to the rope attached to Woc. This was, he convinced himself, just in case Woc got scared and ran off but somehow it gave him a better sense of safety than Woc. Their senses heightened, they made their way deeper into the mountain.

The walls started to become dotted with smaller caves. Like doorways into the mountain. In fact, they looked more like doorways than they did anything else. All were what seemed to be uniform in shape and size and all seemed to be the same distance apart. A squared shaped upright separating them again at a uniform spacing. A fact that none picked up on as they were all too busy being scared to notice. The walls, too, were perfectly flat and had what can only be described as a dusty kind of look to them. Not rounded or rugged like most other cave walls. It was almost as though you could see through them if you looked hard enough. Further they went on and down into the bowels of the mountain. Every now and then, a larger cave entrance, the same size as the one they were in, would shoot off to the left or right leading off into the darkness but they continued forward, not wishing to venture into the uninviting abyss. Karel shone his lantern down one of these tunnels, only to see the light unable to penetrate the blackness and showing no end to the cave. The light being sucked in and swallowed up by the darkness. This bothered Karel more than the others. Karel had a very strange fear for someone who had spent his whole life underground. He was very claustrophobic and hated being closed in! Being on Topside was like heaven for Karel. Even though the terrain was hostile and his chances of survival were slim, at best he loved it! Karel's constant questioning of everything was his attempt to cover up his phobia. To distract people and push them away so that they wouldn't see his fear. He had actually volunteered to join the army rather than wait to be compelled to go. A fact that he hid from everyone except the very confused conscription officer that filled in his application.

A volunteer for Topside! That's a first! he had thought. *No one will believe me when I tell them! Must be running away from something or someone. Yes, that was it. A failed relationship or something more sinister. That can be the only explanation. No one volunteers to go to Topside! Now, quickly get this form done before he asks any more questions!*

Karel had just let him believe whatever he wanted. He just wanted to get out from Below. Had anyone found out why he truly wanted to go, he would have been locked away in a small room of a psychiatric hospital whilst they tried to find out why he hated confined spaces and wanted to venture outside. After all, every Smarian was born and spent most of their lives underground where it was safe. What possessed anyone to want to be outside where it wasn't safe? What was wrong with them? A silly thing to do anyway. To lock someone in a small enclosed room to help cure them when all they wanted to do was escape from being enclosed anywhere! A fate worse than death for Karel. He remembered going to see 'Mad Uncle Dis' as his family had called him. He had been locked away by his own family for feeling the same way. Uncle Dis, who had begged them to be let loose to roam Topside! To get him out from Below! When Karel realised that he, too, hated being at Below, he kept it to himself until he was old enough to do something about it. He hated to have to lie to his uncle and agree with everyone that it was madness to want to be outside. That it was better for Uncle Dis to be locked up than allowed to be free and go to Topside. To lock him away and, as the visits got fewer and fewer, slowly forget that he ever existed. Karel didn't want to be locked away and forgotten like that. Neither did he want his mother and father to suffer the social stigma of having a son diagnosed as being insane! To have people point and stare at them as they walked down the streets. To be dropped from all social circles and watch as their 'friends' one by one slowly disappear. All because their son was different.

Eventually the distant light from outside the cave began to fade as day turned to night, the further they got inside. The light from their lanterns now cocooned them in a bubble that protected them from the weight of the darkness that surrounded them as they made their way onwards. For what seemed like an age in the darkness, they made their way along the amazingly straight route of the cave. A route that never deviated or changed in size. Something that had puzzled Ha'an, the first time he went through it. Made him wonder why nature had been so angular, so smooth and so straight in the formation of these caves. Most other caves were more rugged and round in shape. Going off in all manner of chaotic directions. Much like most other things all around on Topside that nature had formed. Perhaps, the early architects had used the design of these caves when they were building the original streets and buildings of Below, he had thought for they, too, were square and straight! For now though, he was more concerned about getting to the other side than pondering on the caves structure. Something that he knew they wouldn't reach in one day's trek. They would have to camp somewhere along the way and take their chances in the dark. He knew the best place to stop was the great cavern at the centre of the mountain further in. A place where the many other deep dark tunnels that honeycombed the mountain came and went in all directions. A dark echoing chamber but at least it was easy to see if anything approached from any direction. It was also a big enough place for them to rest and try and grab some much-needed sleep whilst taking it in turns to keep watch. To watch for what, he didn't know but thought it safer to do so. Ha'an kept the pace up to reach it as quickly as he could.

It was an hour or so later that Ha'an and the team had made it to where Ha'an thought it would be safe to make camp. The tunnel that they had been travelling along had come to an end at the mouth of the enormous cavern. Huge in size, it seemed as if it was as big as the mountain itself as its roof was way, way up high. They made camp and broke out the rations around the fire, taking some comfort from its warmth and glow. Conversation was scarce and all were constantly looking around this cathedral-like cavern as if expecting something to jump out at them. They had all started to study their strange surroundings and were amazed at what they saw. The walls of the cavern were flat and also peppered with smaller caves as was the entire route from the entrance. All uniform in size and shape as before but now on multiple levels going right up as far as the light would shine. The remains of what looked like pathways going around and up and down the cavern at each level and connecting the doorway like caves to each other. There were also seven other large tunnels at ground level around the cavern, much like the one that they had emerged from leading off into more darkness. Dotted around the caverns vast floor were several tall strangely rectangular shaped rocks rising upwards. These, too, had some form of what looked like writing on them much like the symbols above the entrance. All now faded with age. Smaller similar rocks, again strangely rectangular in shape, laid horizontally on the floor scattered here and there. A very strange place indeed.

"Sergeant Ha'an," Karel whispered inquisitively.

"Yes." replied Ha'an equally as quietly. Neither knowing why they were whispering.

"How do you know which cave to go through to the outside?"

Ha'an thought about his answer. He didn't want to scare them or look silly by saying that all he knew was to go straight on. No one had noticed that he had marked an arrow on the floor when they made camp pointing in the direction to go when they continued on their way. So he decided to expand on the truth a little. Well, quite a lot really!

"Well," he started. "When you've been here as many times as I have, you get to know it quite well. Yes, been here several times with other squads (Once actually!) and on my own (Never!) so I'm pretty used to it by now (NOT!)"

Ha'an looked around at everyone and, as they all seemed to be believing what he was saying, he thought he'd continue on a bit more.

"Yes, I know this place like the back of my hand. Tend to think of it as a bit of an old friend now." he waffled on.

"Sergeant Ha'an. Have you ever met anyone in here? I mean like someone who didn't come with you or was supposed to meet you here?" asked Karel again rather quietly.

"No, can't say I have. Why?" replied Ha'an thinking what a stupid question it was but by now getting quite accustomed to the weird and monumental amount of questions from Karel.

"Well, if we're the only ones in here, yeah, then what's that light doing coming towards us?" Karel was now pointing into the darkness ahead.

"Light?" both Ha'an and Dez shouted at the same time as they both jumped up.

Puzzled as to why they had both jumped up together, Ha'an and Dez looked at each other for a moment. Had Ha'an seen the lights as Dez had seen earlier?

Krun had remained sitting quietly trying to convince himself of a positive in their comment like "it must be help from the base" or "perhaps Tega had found them". Neither comment was helping much. Athan just sat there with a blank expression on his face.

"Yes," Karel continued. "That one, over there!"

They all turned and looked in the direction he was pointing towards and saw the tiniest flicker of what could only be a light of some kind.

"I saw that earlier too but I didn't want to say anything," said Athan very quietly hoping that no one had really heard him.

"Why didn't you say anything?" enquired Karel still trying to keep calm. Not about the light! No, about the way the walls were closing in on him.

"Well, I didn't want to get into any trouble." replied a reluctant Athan.

"Get into any trouble! How much more trouble can we be in? Deep underground with a mountain on top of us in a cavern that's huge and could fall in on us at any moment and…" Karel stopped his rant as the others were now all looking at him very suspiciously rather than at the light.

"When did you say you saw this light?" he continued quickly in a quiet voice trying to shift the emphasis away from himself.

It worked as they were now all on the ground and looking into the distance at the forth coming light.

Ha'an felt everyone's eyes on him as they looked to him for guidance. 'Run!' was his first thought but run to where? Then an ingenious plan hit him.

"Athan!" Ha'an turned towards the quaking hulk. "Go and see what it is!" he commanded.

There was a brief moment of relief from the others and of shock for Athan.

"What? Me? Why?" retorted Athan from under the blanket that he was trying desperately but very unsuccessfully to hide under.

"Because you're the biggest and I said so!" demanded Ha'an in a very almost aggressive voice. Amazing what fear can make you do! He also didn't want to be the one who had to go, so thought this a much better solution!

No one else objected or dared say a word for fear of being picked themselves so a very, very reluctant Athan took his head out from under his blanket.

"Do I really have to go?" pleaded Athan trying his best to look vulnerable with soulful eyes for some kind of sympathy.

A resounding "Yes!" came from all!

"I knew I shouldn't have said anything," whimpered Athan as he got up. One last look down at his colleagues with another attempt at soulful eyes hoping for someone to jump up and say "Don't go!"

No one got up or said a word, just ushered him off.

He let out a huge sigh and, with shoulders hunched, started his way towards the light. Constantly looking back in the hope that they would call him back but no one did.

As soon as he was a good distance away and feeling fairly safe that they wouldn't be asked to go with him, the others moved closer together and watched him disappear into the darkness until all they could see was the light from his lantern.

Athan, for his size, had always suffered from low self-esteem. He had always been mocked for his enormous bulk and, therefore, never really mixed with people because of it. Preferring his own company rather than risk that of others. Not that he wouldn't have minded some friends. He just lacked the confidence to take the first steps to find them. So it was of no surprise to him that he was chosen to go as he had all his life been given tasks that no one else wanted to do. In the past, they had known that he was too scared to stand up for himself and say no. Some had played on his loneliness with the promise of acceptance and friendship if he did what they asked. A false promise and something that had led him into a lot of trouble at school and elsewhere. His father was always putting him down for not standing up for himself and being stupid enough to do the things that he had been goaded into. Calling him all manner of names to only lower his self-belief even more and push him further away from everyone. Hence, his resulted in a very low self-esteem! Not once did he seek help as he thought himself too unimportant for anyone to care.

"Easily lead." had been the thing everyone in authority had said about him. Not once though did anyone ever offer to help him get over it. That was why he had been pleased to receive his call-up papers for the army. To do his national service. If he was always following other people's orders, best he did it in the army where no one knew him and everyone followed orders! Then perhaps he would finally fit in. A fresh start! However, he didn't bank on being sent on a 'special' mission this early in his career!

Even though he had slowed down to the tiniest of steps, the light in the distance was getting closer and closer and he could see that it was approaching him directly. Even when he moved slightly off course, the light changed direction and continued straight towards him. Athan, surrendering to the idea that whatever it was in front of him was going to find him anyway, picked up his step. He pulled himself up to his full height and puffed out his chest. Something that he did rarely for fear of frightening people. His immense physique tensing up a he marched onwards. It felt good for once to be himself at full height and posture and he began to feel a little more confident. Whatever it was out there, he thought, he would tear it apart with his bare hands and show the world just how strong he actually was. "Athan the monster slayer!" they would call him. "Defender of the innocent and hero to all!" he imagined as he marched forward with a renewed vigour.

The light was now very close and Athan could begin to make out an outline in the light. Not sure of what it was, he tried to make himself even bigger than he was. Now, getting so close to the light also brought back the fear but it was too late to go back. Now he had to face whatever it was coming towards him. So close now that he could hear the footsteps of the beast in front of him. His imagination running wild with all the different dangerous things that it could be! How would he survive? Could he even survive? Why didn't he just stay under his blanket and refuse to go? It wasn't like they could have made him go, was it? All this was running through his mind when, to his surprise and great relief, from out of the darkness appeared a beautiful young female Smarian with a huge smile on her face.

"Hello! What are you doing here?" she asked Athan as she continued to approach.

Breathing a huge sigh of relief that she wasn't some kind of murdering monster and now slowly deflating himself down to what he thought as normal size, he replied with great authority. "I'm with them!" and immediately began kicking himself for answering with something quite so dumb!

"Yes," she replied still smiling. "I gathered that but why are you here?"

She was dressed in what looked like army clothes but were much better made. They fitted her exactly where they should and looked very expensive. A very confident person, for most people backed away from Athan on first meeting him because of his sheer size but she had just bounced her way towards him with no fear at all. She was very demure and sporty-looking. Her purple hair tied back to keep it out of the way which exposed her beautiful pale blue complexion. With no visible makeup on her was a very natural beauty. Confident in her own way and giving off an air of intelligence and humility that made Athan feel very comfortable with her. Something that he wasn't used to.

"We're on a special top-secret mission to meet someone called Tega. Something's landed on Topside and we're going to investigate what it is." blurted out Athan. "And I don't think that I was supposed to tell you any of that." he finished annoyed at himself for passing on the information that he really shouldn't have.

"Probably not, but you have now." she said with a little giggle. "I'm Doctor Nerak Catall and I'm not supposed to be here either so I think that makes us even." she replied as if telling him something that she wasn't supposed to say either to make him feel better.

"Now I think we had better go and find the rest of your friends and put their minds at rest, don't you? Bet they didn't expect to find anyone else in here, did they?" And with that, she walked past Athan towards Ha'an and the others beckoning him to follow.

Athan nodded his agreement, turned and they headed off back to the others talking as they went.

Ha'an could see that the lights had met and were now heading towards them. He could only assume that whatever it was that Athan met was friendly and hoped that it would help them out of the darkness of the caves. As they approached, Ha'an hoped that they weren't the same kind of 'lights' that he had encountered on his previous visit. Whilst Dez had talked about the 'lights' that he saw, Ha'an had kept quiet a pooh-poohed the event. Thing being that he, too, had seen the talking 'lights' that Dez had spoken about but had chosen to keep quiet about his encounter with them.

The lights had now got very close and everyone was on edge. Who or what had Athan met in the middle of this vast expanse of nothingness? Were they in danger or salvation? Questions that were about to be answered. No one stirred as closer and closer they came. They could now make out the awesome figure of Athan as he walked towards them with another figure beside him being dwarfed by his size. Athan walked out of the darkness first with his newfound companion at his side. They had become very friendly in during their short stroll towards the others and for some reason, Athan felt very protective of his new friend. Probably down to the fact that Athan hadn't really had any friends before and because she had that effect on most people. Confident and independent whilst feminine but not so vulnerable. As they had got closer, Athan let out a "Hello!" and they all got up to greet him. No one said anything as they both came into view. They were in a state of amazement and disbelief as they saw Athan's newfound friend.

"Hi, I'm Doctor Nerak Catall."

Ha'an shook her outstretched hand and asked the inevitable question. "Who are you and what the hell are you doing down here?"

Nerak shook everyone else's hands as she answered Ha'an's question. "It's a bit of a long story but basically I'm looking for evidence of a lost civilisation." she said and without waiting for a reply, continued. "No one would give me a proper visa to explore out here for what I believe will be the greatest discovery of all time. So instead, I sneaked out on a new recruits transport and jumped off before I got to the base. No one questioned me getting onto the transport as who in their right mind would smuggle themselves to Topside! Smuggle themselves off Topside, yes, but not going to Topside! No one said anything either when I jumped off. Probably thought I was deserting whilst I had the chance! Once off, I met up with an old scout that I had arranged to meet to show me the way to this place and I have been here ever since. About three weeks now. There is so much here that needs exploring and for some reason, the Great Council won't let us do it. I have found so much evidence of an advanced ancient society that it will be hard for them to stop me and others coming out here again, once I publish. Too many archaeologists wanting to know the past and how much they affected our future. Athan has told me of your mission and I would love to come along and help. After all, I do know where I'm going in these caves and can get you out to the other side very quickly." and without waiting for a reply again, she threw off her backpack and sat on the floor beside the fire and said, "Great! We'll leave in a few hours after we have all rested. Have you got anything descent to eat? I'm starving!"

Ha'an and the others were stunned but found themselves all offering Nerak something from their own mediocre rations. All of which were greatly received. They talked for a while and then all tried to get some sleep before they moved on. Nerak slept soundly, at home amongst the darkness and solitude of the caves as the others all just tried their best to relax at least a little bit.

A few hours past and they were all ready to continue their journey through the mountain. Nerak took the lead as the others followed. She was a natural leader and found it very easy to get others to follow her. Her confidence and her determination set her apart from most Smarians and this sometimes put people off her. Her disregard for anyone who said that she couldn't do anything only made her more determined to prove them wrong. A female on Topside alone was totally unheard of so she was out to show that she could and would survive. Ha'an was happy to follow anyone, male or female, who knew a quicker way out of the mountain so he made no objections when she announced that she knew a better path. As they made their way across the vast cavern towards a much smaller tunnel than they had entered through, Ha'an got beside Nerak and asked a question.

"Dr Catall." he started.

"Please call me Nerak," she said, "I find the tittle of doctor a bit pretentious and a little irrelevant on Topside. Here we are all equally at rick from the elements so please call me Nerak."

Ha'an smiled and continued, "Nerak. You say you have been to Topside and in here for three weeks now yet you seem to have survived very well. Haven't you, at any time, been frightened of being here alone?"

Nerak threw him a side glance and asked, "To what am I supposed to be scared of?"

"Well, the unknown, for one thing. You would have had no idea what was out there, let alone what is in here. Didn't you at any time feel that you shouldn't be here or that you weren't alone?"

Ha'an was cautiously looking around just in case something heard him.

"Not really," she replied in a very calm voice. "Why would I be scared of something that hasn't happened yet? As you say, I was alone in here with only my imagination for company and I can see how that could be a fatal mix. If I was to let my imagination run free, I dare say that I could conjure up all sorts of weird and wonderful things to be scared of down here but I don't do things like that. It would be a very silly thing to do with no one around and being somewhere I shouldn't be in the first place, don't you think? No, I just take care that I do the right thing and don't do anything that could harm me. I leave trails for when I'm exploring so that I can find my way back, should I get lost or come to a dead end and as for finding something down here or it finding me…well that would be fantastic!"

Ha'an looked at her in amazement. Whilst what she said made absolute sense, he found it hard to believe that he could tame his fear quite as well as she obviously had.

Nerak continued without looking at Ha'an, "When I first saw your lights in the distance, I thought my luck was in and I was about to see the 'talking lights' that many have proclaimed to have seen and heard."

Luck, was it? Ha'an thought, astounded at her statement as he had been terrified at seeing the 'lights' the first time and certainly didn't want to see them ever again. The thought of someone actually looking for them was beyond his comprehension.

"Well, obviously I made my way towards the lights as quickly as I could and as I got closer to Athan I must admit I thought I was about to meet something that I had never seen before. I mean, after all, he is a very big lad, isn't he? I was a bit disappointed that he was just another Smarian but once he told me about your mission, I got excited again. He isn't in any trouble for telling me, is he? I'd hate to think that he was in trouble for something that he shouldn't have told me. I mean, I would have found you anyway and if you hadn't let me come with you, I would have just followed you anyway." she said in a very flippant way so as not to put the emphasis on what Athan had said.

"No, he's not in any trouble." replied Ha'an. "Tell me more about why you're here. Why do you think that there was an ancient society living here on Topside and if they did exist, where are they now?"

Nerak explained that she and a few others had heard the stories from returning recruits about the wastelands and the weird lights that appeared every now and then and had asked the Great Council to allow them to investigate further. This had been met with a resounding no and they were forbidden to mention it again. This had puzzled them as the Great Council usually had such a laid-back attitude to research of any kind. However, this subject was treated as taboo and a lot of pressure was put on people to forget about it or suffer the consequences. This had been like a red rag to a bull scorse to Nerak and she had made up her mind to investigate, despite what the council had said and to hell with the consequences.

Ha'an had listened intently as they walked along. Not sure whether to tell her about his contact with the 'lights' and what Dez had said about them when he was out there alone. How they had talked to him of the past and the future. It definitely gave him something other than the darkness to think about.

A few hours later and they were all very relieved to see a spec of light in the distance. Well, once Nerak had told them that it was the way out, they were relieved. They certainly didn't want it to be anything other than the way out! The pace quickened. Then gradually the spec became a spot and then a dot as closer they got. It wasn't long before they could see the daylight streaming into the cave and the pace hotted up even more. Almost running, they all emerged from the mountain and sank to the floor and bathed in the sunlight. None more relieved than Karel, for obvious reasons. All, except Nerak. She was already looking to see in what direction they were heading and wondering whether she would find the answers to the questions she had.

Chapter 9
The Information Bureau

Asil felt very pleased with herself as she waltzed into her office building that morning. She finally had the proof that she had always been looking for. Proof that things were really landing on Smar and the Great Council, as well as the Great One himself, were keeping it a secret. Finally she would be exemplified for the previous times she made the claims that things weren't as they were supposed to be on Topside. This time she had the definite proof from a council official that there were objects landing on Smar. That the Great Council not only knew about it but had actively made sure that it remained a secret. The objects that had landed had been moved to a secret location that the Great Council publicly denied existed and were being examined by a team of top scientists to find out what they were and where they came from. The fact that they came from somewhere other than Smar would be of great concern and spark many a question. What else was out there in the night sky and why had they come to Smar? Were they from a friendly species or were these objects the beginning of an invasion of Smar? Was Smar about to be enlightened by a superior race as to the wonders of the universe or be enslaved by a tyrannical advanced race that would rape the planet of all its natural resources and destroy all in its path? Questions that needed answers but not one of these immeasurably important questions had even entered Asil's head! All she sought was the acclaim that such a discovery would bring. This time she would be vindicated from all the past comments of her making it up and seeking fame by fiction. Either way, she was about to destroy the belief that most Smarians had that the lights in the dark sky were portholes from the next world where their ancestors spirits looked down at them from time to time. Where they all moved on to when their physical bodies had given up in this world. The clerics definitely wouldn't be happy! Out of their comfortable job for life and the comfortable lifestyle that went with it. Preaching to the people how to live their lives whilst not always living up to the high standards they set themselves. Sweeping any scandal regarding a cleric under the carpet. Never openly admitting that any crime had been committed. Covering for each other and blasting all those who thought different.

Briefcase in hand, she climbed the stairs to her editor's office and redemption! She had a spring in her step and a smile on her face. As she passed all the other reporters diligently working away on the smaller insignificant stories of the day, she felt even more important than ever. If that was indeed possible, for she had always had an inflated view of herself anyway!

No one looked at her as she passed as deep in their own little worlds they were immersed. No one and no story was more important than what they were working on. Their entire world, at that moment in time, was completely taken up with them and their report. There was no room for anyone else and that was probably why most of them were single. No time or place for relationships outside of the bubble that was work. Everything came a poor second to the story and how it might propel their career into the high life and the fame that they sought so blindly. No thought for the old and burnt out reporters that had spent their entire life looking for 'THE' story to take them up into the limelight but only to find themselves in the backlight of life itself. Never living life at all, only existing for the possible that was more often improbable and was never going to happen for them. Not that they would ever believe you, even if you could get a minute of their time to try and explain it to them. For them, it was something that they sort for above all else. Blinkered from everything else that was considered normal and moral by other Smarians, they would delve into the lives of others. To expose any dark secret, however personal without any regard to their victims feelings and privacy. A 'good' story often failed to protect the innocent merely expose their naivety. The occasional story would bring those in power to answer questions that they would have preferred were never asked. Usually though, they would just melt into the background without answering. More of a tactical retreat than justice itself. It could be months before they would raise their heads again when the papers and the people had moved on to a more 'interesting' story about someone else!

At the top of the stairs was the lavish office of the editor. Asil brushed past the attentions of the editor's secretary with a "He's waiting for me!" as the secretary tried to stop her. She opened the door with great purpose and walked into the middle of the office as if she owned it. Something that she was already aiming for.

The office was full of pictures of so-called celebrities at various venues, all happily smiling away and shaking hands with the editor. The smiles were generally fake as half the time they had no idea who he was. Just someone that their agent said it would be a good idea to have their picture taken with as it could be good for publicity. They all went along with it as the celebrity industry was a cauldron of fake smiles and friendships. The more famous they were, the more people proclaimed to be their 'friend'. When the fame stopped for whatever reason their so-called 'friends' disappeared too as many had found in the past and many more would do in the future. By looking around at all the pictures in the office, this editor had a lot of 'friends'!

There were two big comfortable chairs in front of the editor's desk which he would beckon all who came in to sit in. There were there for two reasons for this. One to make the visitor feel at ease and hopefully lower their guard. The other reason was that the editor was quite a small Smarian and he had both chairs lowered so that he could look down on whomever was sitting in them, giving himself a feeling of power. His desk was enormous, too, so as to signify his standing on the paper. This was something that every reporter had become aware of over the years and all had become very wary of the editor when he asked them to sit down in either chair with a smile on his face. Asil was very aware of this, too, and made a point of never sitting down in his office. She preferred to strut up and down the office to declare that she was in control and, this, she did again.

Zab, the editor, sat back in his chair with an arrogant look of disgust as she bowled in.

"What do you want?" he asked, barely moving. He was good at barely moving. It was something that he had perfected over the years of dealing with single-minded journalists. He found that it unnerved them when they came into his office and demanded things. If he didn't move, then they were never sure if they had his attention, which was generally why they barged into his office in the first place. Other than that he barely moved because he was somewhat rotund and found it difficult to move that quickly anyway but he liked his version why he did it better than the truth! He looked the part too. Although his clothes were expensive, his wife insisted on it, they hung on him in such a way that they looked scruffy. Fitting for a world of deceit and deception. Long since making the move from reporter to editor via a big scandal that he had discovered, embellished a bit, quite a bit, and then reaped the rewards of this biased and unyielding world of 'news' by destroying yet another person's life and career.

"I've got the proof!" Asil announced and slammed down the Herald's paperwork on Zab's desk.

Unperturbed Zab didn't even bat an eyelid which wasn't hard as Smarians didn't have eyelids!

"Proof of what?" he asked as if not caring. Leaning forward slightly and looking over his glasses but not touching the documents that Asil had thrown onto his desk.

"Proof that the Great Council have known for a long while that strange things have been happening on Topside for years and have kept it quiet. That they DO have a secret place where they keep things and experiment on them. A place that they would definitely prefer that no one in the public domain ever knew about. Why, even now they have sent a team to go and investigate something else that has recently landed Topside!" Asil announced with great passion.

Zab slowly picked up the documents giving Asil a very dismissal glance. He was too long in the tooth to believe every young reporter's claim to a substantial story. He had heard them all over his very long and despicable career. He had no preconceptions as to what a 'good' or 'bad' story was any more, as long as it sold newspapers. Long gone was his sense of right and wrong that he had started his career within his early naive days of journalism. Now it was all about who was deceiving who and for what. The truth was sometimes something that just got in the way of a good story nowadays. Asil waited patiently as he glanced through the paperwork thrown onto his desk. Nervously, she waited and trying desperately to keep herself from talking whilst he read knowing that he loathed impatience in a reporter.

"Wait until I've read the facts before you start to interrupt me!" was his usual retort to all of those that tried to rush him.

Asil was barely holding it together as he eventually looked up over his glasses again and slumped back into his big chair.

"Looks like you might have something here," he said in a very calm voice. "The Herald? Does he know you took these documents from his briefcase?"

Asil was stopped from answering with a wave from his two left hands dismissing his own question.

"I don't want to know where or how you got this information. I don't suppose, for one minute, that the Herald knowingly gave you these documents and I certainly don't want to be implicated in any possible investigation, if there ever is one. Just make sure that you write a good story and stick to the detail in the documents. I don't want any speculation about what it means or what they are investigating. The public will make up enough of their own stories without any help from you. Just that they have something on Topside that makes them nervous, okay?"

Asil nodded her acceptance and Zab threw the documents back at her.

"I want it done by the end of the day! I don't want to have to go explaining myself to the Great Council if they notice these documents are missing before the story hits the evening papers. You understand?"

Again Asil nodded as she picked up the papers and backed out of the editor's office. The grin on her face almost made her face ache. The secretary glared at her as she passed but nothing was going to spoil this moment for Asil. As she moved outside the office, another young, very keen reporter tried to enter and was met with a tirade of abuse and sent packing before they had even said a word. Asil smiled as she had been there before. A disheartened rookie passed her with head bowed as she meandered her way back to her desk to write the story that was going to re-launch her career. All manner of things running through her head. The parties she would have to attend. The interviews she would give. Perhaps even a chat show or two or three!

Big time, here we come! she thought as she sat down to type.

Unbeknown to Asil in her own little world of self-fulfilment, she had not spotted the small Smarian male who had followed her from the bar the previous night. He had trailed her to her paper's offices and had waited for her to go in before changing direction and heading towards the Great

Chambers. Not for him, though the great entrance. No, he chose a very different path down a side alley and in through a very unimportant looking door leading to the inner chambers. This was his usual entrance away from the prying eyes of the tourists and photographers hoping to get a glimpse of the Great One himself. Once inside, he made his way through the maze of dark narrow corridors. They were very ordinary and neglected unlike the splendour of the Great Chambers and its surrounding offices. There were no pictures adorning these walls and no windows either. The paint was dull and peeling in places and they looked as if they had been painted an aeon ago. No carpet either. Just plain wooden floors all gnarled up with age and the constant clandestine traffic. He doubted whether the Great One even knew that these offices existed or cared. No one said anything to him as he passed them along the way. No one said anything to anyone down here. Barely a glance between them in acknowledgement of their existence as they passed by. All were involved in some form of skulduggery or other and kept themselves to themselves. The offices down here were small and badly lit. Doors slammed closed as soon when anyone passed by or tried to look into them. Such was the distrust within this hive of the unseen. For this was the world of the infamous 'Information Bureau'. Here they collected information about everyone and everything. From a birth to a death, a school exam to a degree, a marriage or a divorce. All information about every Smarian's daily life, no matter how mundane or exciting it may be, was kept on file and recorded, just in case one day it could be of use. Not that anyone knew about it. No, the majority of Smarians had never heard of the Information Bureau let alone what its job was. And that was exactly how the few people that knew of and ran the department wanted it. Its sordid little world was kept well away from the attention of the Smarian people. Those unfortunate few that did come into contact with this department rarely got to tell their tale for fear of the consequences which could be very, very severe!

Mr Tash continued his way along the corridor to the end where a large door was to be found. It looked more than a little bit out of place to all the other doors. Well maintained and highly polished with a bright light breaking free into the corridor from its underside. He knocked on the door and waited for an answer.

"Come in," spoke a very authoritative voice after a while and in went Mr Tash.

It was like traversing to different worlds as he went through the doorway to the office beyond. Gone was the badly lit corridor full of dens of iniquity and Smarians that were more like shadows on the walls as they moved around. Their nick name of 'spectres' well deserved! Now Mr Tash was standing in the very well lit, very splendidly furnished office of the 'Information minister'. The walls were adorned with pictures of the minister and other VIPs at all manner of important functions, much like the General's office. Everything in the office was grand. From the furniture to the picture frames, no expense had been spared. The big desk from which the voice had emanated was made from the finest wood and was so highly polished you could see your face in it! Not that Mr Tash looked at his reflection, if he could help it. After all, the things that he had seen and done he didn't always like to be reminded that he, too, was a Smarian. Not one Smarian would do all that he had done in his long career as an information officer and look at himself in the mirror without regret. Hence he didn't look in the mirror and so could continue to do what he was good at. Snooping! Or rather 'information gathering' to give it its official term. Snooping to the rest of us! A bit like the journalist that he had been following but at a much higher and official level.

"Well?" asked the voice inquisitively from a very large chair. Mr Tash could only see the back of the chair as the door that he came through was hidden well away in the corner of the office. He moved slowly around the walls of the office towards the side of the desk and spoke.

"I'm afraid that we may have a bit of a situation, sir."

"Go on," the voice from the chair sounding interested.

Mr Tash moved further around the edge of the office until he could almost see who was sitting in the chair.

"You see, sir, I think that the Herald has been compromised by that very annoying yet very pretty journalist," said Mr Tash gradually sliding his way around the office and desk surveying the office as he went. Sticking as closely to the wall as possible. He didn't like being in the brightness of the office and hated being the centre of anyone's attention. He was more at home in the dark corners away from everyone's view whilst keeping all in his!

"Which one?" spoke the voice from the chair. "I find them all very annoying!"

"The one from the past year or so, who threatened to expose the landings, sir. Got one of the troops to talk about that fatal mission where most of the recruits didn't make it back. He got sent to Topside indefinitely for…"

"Yes, yes, I know the story! What has she done this time?" the voice had cut Mr Tash short.

By now, Mr Tash had slivered and sidled his way around towards the front of the desk and could finally see the information minister in his chair.

"Will you please stop creeping around my office and tell me what has gone on!" the minister said as he put his pen down and focused on Mr Tash. "You really annoy me when you do that!"

Mr Tash looked completely out of place in this environment. His grey drab clothing helped him stay unseen in the background of the streets and alleys of Below. His slim build and pale complexion, an asset for the dark corners where he sat, listened and observed others who are unaware of who he was and what he did. 'Spectre' suited him and his colleagues. But here in the splendour of the minister's office, he stood out like a sore thumb! The backdrop of bright colours which most Smarians loved surrounded him like an unwanted blanket. The minister's fine clothes, the absolute opposite of his own.

"It would seem, sir, that this journalist has duped the Herald into thinking that she would publish his poetry and, after a well-planned distraction, whilst he wasn't looking, stole some documents from his briefcase that he so stupidly had with him," continued Mr Tash.

"Poetry?" inquired the minister.

"Yes, sir." replied Mr Tash. "It would seem that the Herald believes himself to be somewhat of a poet. I have read some of his work and I must admit that although it's not really my thing, he really is quite good."

"You've read some of his work?" a somewhat astonished minister retorted.

"Oh yes, sir. I considered it part of my job to see what the Herald was writing about in his little diary that he keeps with him all the time. I was curious to see if there was anything in it that could be seen as harmful to the Great Council so I watched him as he sat in his usual place of writing. Have been doing it ever since I knew he was writing things down, sir." answered Mr Tash.

"Poetry? The Herald? How do you know it's poetry if he keeps the book with him all the time? Does his wife know? Where's his usual place of writing?" The minister was full of questions.

"Well, sir," started Mr Tash, "no, his wife doesn't know. Don't think he has ever had the nerve to tell her and I don't blame him. Scary woman. Always at functions and lunches trying to be more than she is. If she found out, the scandal would kill her. No. No, she would probably kill him just to stop the scandal! His usual place of writing is the men's room. Third cubicle on the left. Always the same cubicle for some reason. Never worked out why? Very hard to get a mirror in there to see what he was writing without him finding out I can tell you. Got some very strange looks! Yes, indeed. Got it perfected now though."

The minister's mind for a moment flashed a picture of the Herald on the loo and Mr Tash with a mirror before he thankfully dismissed the thought as a bad idea. A shiver of disgust running down his spine.

"I take it that the story hasn't been run yet?" the minister said, regaining his composure.

"No, sir, not yet," Mr Tash replied. "I believe that she is writing it up as we speak, sir. Will probably try and get it in the evening paper if I know Zab. Oh, the editor, sir. Yes, know him well. I have had many dealings with him over the years, sir. Slippery little customer. Often thought that he would make an excellent information officer, sir."

"I think that we ought to have a quiet word with this Zab fellow, don't you? Best we go to him rather than give him the chance to be 'out' when we request his presence here. Plus I don't think that we really need a member of the press visiting the Information Bureau. Might give them some misguided idea that we were keeping an eye on everyone. Can't have people thinking that the Great Council are watching their every movement now, can we? Not good for the image of the Great One! Not that he knows anything about it anyway!" and with that minister, started to laugh.

Mr Tash joined in with an unnerving little snigger much more suited to him than a laugh. The minister got up out of his impressive chair and moved towards the coat stand. He took off his bright red jacket and donned the dark grey coat and hat of an information officer. Now he, too, looked out of place in the splendour of his own office. His face took on a more serious look and his whole stature seemed to change. He began to look more like Mr Tash than a minister from the Great Council. Transition completed, they both moved towards the door whence Mr Tash first arrived, down the narrow corridors and out of the building.

Chapter 10

The Machines

Tega wasn't normally pleased to see anyone out on topside but this time he was pleased to see the dust cloud that could only mean that the investigating team were close by. He made his way towards them faster than he would normally move. He had spent the last few days watching those damned machines and for once in his life had been looking forward to having the company of other Smarians. He could make out the recruits as they approached. Five soldiers of all shapes and sizes, probably new recruits as always, the obligatory scorse and…a female! Whilst it was not unusual to have a female recruit but by her attire Tega knew that she was not in the Smarian army!

Was she one of those scientists from 'THE' place? he wondered. *Surely not someone from the Information Bureau? No, she looked far too normal for one of them. Too well dressed and far too pretty,* he thought.

He knew about the Information Bureau as it had been them that had put him on Topside in the first place. He hadn't heeded their warnings about his radical thoughts of politics for the people and not just for the Great Council and its favourites. Why shouldn't the people have a say in the daily running of Below? Why was it that only a select number of people were 'elected' to the Great Council by the Great Council and not by the people? These thoughts that he voiced very publicly whenever he could were his crime that got him to Topside years ago. Whilst he waited for them to draw closer, he began reminiscing about the night that the 'spectres' called for him.

They arrived late one night to inform Tega that he was to be sent to Topside for training right away, for the sake of his family and friends who might become contaminated by his unSmarian-like thoughts. Unlike the other times when there had been just one or two of them that had appeared late at night to 'discuss' with him that he should change his ways and conform more to the Smarian way of thinking, this time there were five of them. All dressed in the usual drab grey coats and hats that was the dress code of the spectres. One, whose name Tega would never forget, Mr Tash, seemed to have great joy in reading the order from the Great Council sending him to Topside for 'rehabilitation' for a year…or so. The others just seemed devoid of all emotion as they waited to lead him off into the night and to an uncertain future. Tega remembered the look of disappointment on his father's face. The many father and son chats that they had about keeping Tega's ideas to himself and not voicing them to all and sundry and thereby bringing himself to the attention of the notorious Information Bureau, all gone to waste. The arguments after the spectres' first and subsequent visits had brought much bad feeling between them. Tega dismissed his father's arguments out of hand as that of an old Smarian who had been indoctrinated by the Great Council and its lies. Whilst he was right about the indoctrination tactics of the Great Council, he couldn't see how his father was just trying to save his son from being taken away and thrown to the elements on Topside. As with most youngsters, Tega thought he knew best and paid no heed to his father's words which in hindsight were to come true. Little did he know that his father was talking from experience from when he was a young man. He had seen with his own eyes what happened to young men who tried to rebel too much against the Great Council. He had friends that had held the same radical thoughts as Tega and knew what happened to them. They disappeared!

His mother just sobbed uncontrollably as Tega was marched out of the door and out of their lives, probably forever. The young man that she had so many hopes for, that she was so proud of, now being dragged away into the night. She desperately clung onto his brother and sister who, bemused by what was happening and too young to comprehend why their mother was crying, just waved him goodbye as they did every day. Not knowing that this was the last that they would see of their elder brother. He hadn't given in easily though. He struggled at first to get away but when he saw how this just made things worse for his family, now all crying and hugging each other, he stopped and accepted his fate. Taking a last look at his home and family as he was transported off to the world that he now called home. Later, he could have lied and said that his time on Topside had changed him and that he no longer believed in his hopes for a democratic free and fair Below. He could but didn't because he hadn't lost any of his rebellious ideas and his time on Topside just made him more bloody-minded. This and all manner of things were running through his mind as they approached.

Ha'an could make out a figure coming towards them and assumed rightly that it was Tega. Who else would it be out here in the wilderness? A brief moment of relief engulfed him before he realised that it must also mean that they were now perilously close to whatever it was that had landed on Smar. With mixed emotions, Ha'an rushed towards Tega with a smile on his face and shook Tega's hands. He had heard about Tega and realised that a salute was out of the question. Just as he was about to exchange pleasantries Ha'an stopped as he saw the look on Tega's face.

"Who is she and why is she here?" demanded Tega in a voice loud enough so that Nerak could hear.

"She has a name and it's Nerak!" stated Nerak in a very calm but firm way. She was used to Smarian males not liking her forthright manner and so wasn't fazed by Tega's reaction to her. Some Smarian males could be very intimidated by her confidence as most females were taught not to compete with the males. To react almost subservient to their male counter parts. Nerak clearly didn't agree with nor go along with this idea.

"And where did you come from? I suppose you just happened to come across these recruits in the middle of Topside, did you?" Tega replied in a very sarcastic manner.

"Well, actually I found them in the middle of a mountain whilst I was surveying it for signs of ancient life. Found some too! They were a little bit lost so I showed them a quicker way out of the mountain as I knew the terrain better than they did." she replied in an equally condescending manner and showing off at the same time. "They mentioned their little expedition to see what had landed on Smar and I decided to come along with them. They didn't have much choice either as if they hadn't let me tag along with them then I would have just followed on behind. So you see, this is why I am here and as for the who I am, well, I am the daughter of the Minister of Foreign Affairs."

"Foreign Affairs?" blurted out Tega. "We don't have any foreign affairs?"

Tega was somewhat confused as to what a foreign affair was. He wasn't alone as all of the others had thought the same thing but hadn't said anything for fear of looking stupid. You see, as there were only Smarians on Smar and they all lived together at Below and there were no 'foreigners' to have affairs with! A bit like the army really. As there were no enemies and no wars there really was no purpose in having an army. However, the Great Council in its infinite wisdom deemed that they should have one, just in case. In case of what, no one knew or dared ask but it did give the Great Council a chance to give a few more 'select' Smarians good jobs! It was just as well really that there were no enemies to fight as the Smarian army had no weapons to fight with anyway! The fact that Nerak had also said that she was the daughter of this 'Foreign Affairs' minister had just gone straight over everyone's head!

"I know!" replied Nerak. "Never could work out what it meant either. Just a title to make it sound more official rather than 'jobs for the boys', I think. Mind you, it did give me access to all the best schools and teachers. Gave me the chance to study under professor Snikwah and learn more about his theories of life on Topside aeons ago. Really quite an eye opener and even though he has now been locked away for publishing his book *A brief history of the origins of Smarians*, I found myself compelled to seek proof and vindicate him. Hence I'm on Topside. Now when can we go and see the landing site?"

Tega was taken aback by Nerak much as most males were. Her forwardness was only matched by her beauty. She was very much the tomboy and had always got on better with males than females. Not for her playing with dolls with her sisters. She was out exploring and playing sports with the boys. Something that had always got her into trouble with her parents and teachers all through her childhood and on through to university. Now she was a very independent female with a mind of her own. Something else that the Smarian society didn't encourage.

Tega looked once more at Ha'an who just shrugged his shoulders and smiled. He had become accustomed to Nerak's attitude and found it somewhat refreshing. Plus he knew that it was pointless to argue with her. She had already told him that the reason he didn't understand her point of view was that he was wrong and until he realised that, agreed that what she said made sense as she was right, then there was no point in arguing about it! There was logic in there somewhere but it just eluded Ha'an for the moment. Well, so she told him anyway.

"Well, er, I suppose," began Tega before he was interrupted by Nerak.

"Good! Let's eat first and make our way there after a brief rest. I'm starving again." and with that they all sat down and began to eat.

Tega, for once, was gobsmacked and after a brief moment of rebellion, well, he just mumbled to himself whilst everyone ate, he found himself just accepting the situation and getting on with it. Besides, he was hungry too.

Nerak sat among them and talked about her time studying under the tuition of Professor Snikwah and how he thought that all life originated from Topside. How there had been great cities built there and the remnants were there to be seen if only people would look. As to why they disappeared, he didn't know but thought that by studying the remains, it might give them some idea of what happened and where they went. Hence she had been in the mountain as she believed that it had once been some kind of a gathering place for the ancient Smarians. A super huge marketplace of sorts where they would shop for all manner of things. Lots of different places side by side selling different goods. Not too unlike the high streets of Below, just on a grander scale. She told how Professor Snikwah had spoken of the missing history of the beginnings of Smar and how much more was known by a select few but never revealed. Something that for some reason the Great Council forbade saying that it was a silly idea and only a madman would even consider such things. Hence, Professor Snikwah was deemed to be mad for having such thoughts and, as he was trying to encourage others to believe the same, he was locked up! The young recruits listened to her intensely but were not really paying much attention to what she was saying. With her soft, silky voice, she could have been talking about the mating habits of a scorse and they would still have listened just as intensely. Such was the way she had with the boys.

Lunch finished, they all prepared to move towards the landing site. It was half a day's walk to the site and Tega had been telling them how he first saw it land. He gave them all the details about when and how it landed and how he had grabbed the piece with the markings on to give his story the proof he would need to get the commandant to believe him. He told them everything except for the thing that even he found hard to believe. That he would let them find out for themselves for they would never believe him otherwise. He wasn't even sure that he believed what he saw. After all, that was impossible, wasn't it?

As they approached the landing site, Dez tied Woc to a rock and gave him something to eat to keep him amused. Dez was becoming immune to the side-effects of feeding Woc by now. Much to the others' disgust as they all made sure that they were well away from them both, before the feeding started. With a pat on the head for Woc whilst quietly saying, "Be good and I'll be back soon," Dez made his way to join the others. Tega had cautioned them to remain very quiet as he had no idea if the machine would be wandering around. Something that they were prone to do during the daylight hours. He also had no idea if the machines could hear them at all but thought it best not to try and prove that they could. As they made their way through the maze of rocks towards the site, a great sense of apprehension gripped them all. Tega was at the front with Nerak close behind him. Ha'an and the others weren't so keen to get there or be so near to the front. Athan brought up the rear as Tega didn't want to risk him being seen and give everyone away. Athan had no complaints about this at all! It was the first time that he was actually pleased that his size made him different. They came to the top of the hill and Tega pointed towards the landing site and described what they could see. Sure enough, there was the object from which the machines had first emerged plus the other much larger structure which the machines had erected. Now they had added to this an even stranger structure. Enormous in size, it took up most of the site. Glass-like in appearance but still in a domed shape. Inside, they had row upon row of some strange green treelike things. Similar to the bright red postlethwaite trees of the forest of Ebb. These green things were tended to every day by the machines and great care was taken with them. They were kept under some strange yellow light and were fed with what looked like water on a regular basis. Tega had observed that there was an inner and an outer doorway that the machines had to go through before entering these domed structures but he had no idea why. He didn't tell them what the machines did when they got past the inner doorway. That they would have to see for themselves! There were various objects of different shapes and sizes scattered all around the central structure. Tega explained how the machines moved around each of these objects with great care. Some were examined everyday whilst some like the massive upside-down dome was just left alone. Only on occasion did it move itself by swivelling around on its sole supporting spike to point in another direction and stay there doing nothing. What purpose this performed was beyond Tega. He had merely observed what went on. There was a silence amongst the group as Tega explained how he watched the machines everyday digging in the dust for something. Taking samples back inside a smaller dome structure with only the one flimsy door. One of the machines would operate a strange contraption that drilled its way into the ground deeper and deeper every day. How the machines would look at what was coming out of the ground with great interest only to continue drilling further down. Its purpose unknown. Tega could only guess that that it was looking for water but he knew that you wouldn't find any water there. Water wasn't found in this part of Topside. It was only found to the north and the south, the remotest parts of Smar where the great uninhabited subterranean frozen wastelands were. Where the frozen glaciers of ice melted to form the cold seas of fresh water that slowly meandered their way down to the city of Below via the many lakes and rivers. Thankfully they were nowhere near Below either. Who knows what would happen if they drilled all the way down into below itself? The Great Council would have a real problem trying to explain that away. A new express way to Topside, perhaps?

Nothing much happened for ages as Tega continued to explain that sometimes the machines didn't leave the two main structures. Then they all began to feel it. It was only a slight feeling to begin with. A slight tingling through their bodies as they lay on the ground. Everyone looked at each other and then all looked to Tega. He shrugged his shoulders and told them that he had never this sensation before in all his years at Topside. Then the tingling became a shaking and then the whole ground started to move. They all held on tightly, not knowing what was happening. Fear in their hearts as the ground beneath them shook with a terrible force. A Smarquake perhaps? Suddenly they found out what it was that was happening for passing close by them came a massive machine like nothing they had ever seen before. It was enormous! Almost as big as the two main structures but this one was moving! It had four, no six giant wheels supporting some sort of large bubble and in that bubble sat the two machines side by side. Plastered with the same kind of markings found on all the other structures and objects, it made its thunderous way towards the landing site leaving a trail of upturned ground as it went. Throwing clouds of red dust and rocks into the air as it moved along shaking the ground. It made some kind of high-pitched whining noise as it moved onwards coming to a stop just outside the structures. Ha'an shivered with fear as he recognised the noise from his previous experience with the much smaller machine that had killed his old compatriots. However, this machine was much, much bigger.

With the ground now still, Tega and Nerak looked up to observe this massive machine that had passed them far too close for comfort. The others just stayed huddled on the floor not wanting to look or move. Tega and Nerak watched as both the machines exited the bubble and moved to the back of this wheeled monster. Here they collected huge bags of rocks and what looked like a glass container with something moving around in it. They took them all into the smaller domed structure and closed the door. The machine with the wheels stood silent. Without the other two machines inside, it was silent and stationery. Everyone breathed a sigh of relief. That had been close. Too close! Thinking that this had been enough observing for the day, and the fact that they had been scared silly, the group moved back and decided that they should set up camp further away. Much further away!

On the way, Tega and Ha'an had decided that a lookout would have to be posted as soon as they made camp to alert the others, just in case the machine started moving again. A pointless decision made out of fear as they wouldn't have been able to sleep through the noise and vibration anyway! Not even Krun, who loved his sleep, would be able to sleep through that. They came to the spot where Dez had tied up Woc and all that was left was the rope. Dez thought that the silly scorse had broken loose and just wandered off and started to look for him. Calling his name as he went. The others made camp as best they could whilst making derogatory comments about Dez's rope tying skills. Dez followed Woc's tracks away from the camp hoping that he was nearby. He didn't fancy going too far away from the others after today's events. Fortunately though it was in the opposite direction from the landing site!

Suddenly Dez came to a stop. He hadn't found Woc but what he did find wasn't very encouraging. Woc's tracks had just stopped and what replaced them was very worrying. Huge marks in the ground, the size of Woc, took over from where Woc's tacks had stopped. Dez continued on following these enormous markings. He didn't want to but he needed to know what had happened to his friend and this drove him on. Anxious and scared, he slowly pushed on until they too disappeared giving way to even bigger troughs in the ground. The troughs disappeared in both directions but Dez had recognised what these troughs had been made by. He had seen them earlier. He had seen them being made by that huge moving monster. Woc had been taken by the machines! He sank to the ground and cried out "No!" at the top of his voice.

Tega looked at Ha'an as they all heard Dez's scream. They dropped what they were doing and bolted in the direction of the scream. Not fearing as to why he had screamed, just anxious to find out. They found Dez kneeling on the floor sobbing for his Woc. Neither knew what to do until Nerak arrived and, realising what must have happened, fell to the floor and hugged Dez trying desperately to console him. Tega and Ha'an looked at the troughs leading back to the landing site. They realised now that the machines must have taken their scorse. He had been the thing moving around in that glass container. This left them with a dilemma. They knew that they needed that scorse to power their equipment. Without him, nothing worked. They had to decide what to do. Whether to go back to base camp without the means to communicate with anyone or power their lanterns. These they would desperately need to go through the mountain. Without them would mean going the long way around and would take them at least another two maybe three weeks extra. Leaving them exposed to the elements of Topside and running out of rations. Or they could decide to get their scorse back somehow. They headed back to camp with Dez still being consoled by Nerak. Tega and Ha'an sat around the fire and explained the situation and the choice they would have to make.

"We have to go and get Woc!" pleaded Dez. "He saved my life and I am not going back without him!"

Nerak put her left arms around him again to console and support him.

"Beside which I don't much fancy going back through that mountain again without any lanterns and the long way around could kill us all if we get caught in another storm!"

Karel backed him up on this, for he didn't want to go back through the mountain again at all! Let alone without any lanterns! He didn't, however, mind staying out on Topside for three more weeks though but he didn't think it prudent of him to say so!

"I vote we go and get our scorse back," said Nerak. "We need him, Dez needs him and it would be VERY exciting! Us against the machines! We would return as heroes that fought the machines and triumphed. You'd all get promoted and I

135

would get the recognition that I need to start a legitimate search on Topside. What do you say, guys?"

Not impressed by her unbelievable excitement of taking on the machines, the others all came up with good reasons to go back to base and to go and get their scorse back. It was left to Tega and Ha'an to decide. They pondered on the pros and cons of each scenario for quite a considerable amount of time and eventually came up with a decision and a plan. Tega was the first to talk.

"We have decided to rescue the scorse!" he reported to them.

Dez let go a huge sigh of relief without thinking about the consequences of that decision.

"The forecast was for more storms so going back around the mountain is out of the question if we are all to survive. So, that just leaves us with the problem of getting the scorse back."

The others all looked at each other and then back at Tega. They were caught between a rock and a hard place. Damned if they did and damned if they didn't.

"However, I do have a plan." said Tega and beckoned them all to gather closer.

"I have a good idea after watching them for so long where they will be keeping him. The small dome where they keep taking all the samples. I think I saw them take him there in a glass container when we saw them arrive in that damn wheeled machine. All we have to do is wait until they've gone out in their bubble machine, break into the dome, find the scorse, free him and get back before they return!"

Tega sat back with a pleased grin on his face. The master plan now revealed.

"That's it?" questioned Nerak.

"Yes," replied Tega not sure why his great plan was being questioned.

"Just wait until they've gone and sneak in?" Nerak said in a more than slightly unimpressed way.

"Just like that!" replied Tega confidently.

"Okay then," replied Nerak unconvinced that this was the best plan. However, in the absence of any other plan she was willing to take her chances after all, what's an adventure without risks?

"When do we leave?"

"At first light. They won't move now before then," replied Tega and he began spelling out when and how they were going to liberate the scorse. No one was totally convinced about Tega's plan but as no one had come up with a better one, and they really did try, they all went along with it. As they lay in their tents that night, no one really got much sleep. All were conscious about the risks that they were about to take the following morning.

Whilst all this was going on, no one had noticed the two lights hovering around behind them. They had been there for quite some time observing what was going on.

"Is this the moment of first contact?" enquired the smaller one.

"No. That doesn't happen for years yet," replied the other one. "This is just before they realise that they are not alone in this universe. But first contact, no. They don't even know what these 'machines' as they put it are or where they come from yet. Just keep watching and all will be revealed."

"Can't I just speak to them and find out more about it now rather than wait until later?" asked the smaller one somewhat impatiently.

"No! You know the rules. No contact to be made at all. We can't have you and the other students messing around with time now, can we? There are already Smarians of this time period talking about us as 'lights in the sky' as it is. We don't want to create more panic now, do we? Just watch and listen. You know there's a test afterwards, don't you?" said the larger one in a very authoritative voice.

"I hate history!" declared the smaller one and did as it was told. Quietly and without anyone noticing they watched and observed.

Chapter 11

Ministers and Messengers

Zab was sitting in his office trying to read a small book on how to make friends, written by a little-known female author called Ayrm Yelhind. It had been given to him by his wife the previous evening as she was fed up of him having no friends at all, apart from the many journalists and minor celebs trying to suck up to the editor. Zab had tried to object but thought better of it as it travelled through the air and hit him on the head. He may have been the big powerful editor of a major newspaper during the day, but at home he was just the husband. Zab had thought about giving it to someone else to read on his behalf but knew that he would be quizzed about it later and didn't want to suffer the consequences of being found out. Just as he was turning over yet another dull page of self-opinionated, intellectual twaddle, his secretary poked her head around the door and coughed to get his attention.

"What is it?" barked Zab even though he was only too pleased for any reason to stop having to read the book. He still barked though as he didn't want to change his image of a grumpy obnoxious editor.

"You have a visitor," she replied very quietly and politely.

"I don't have time for any visitors," barked Zab again. "Tell them to take a running…"

He was stopped midsentence as through his door walked the Information minister with Mr Tash lurking behind him.

"I feel sure that you have time for me," announced the minister as he pushed past the secretary and ushered her away with a wave of his hand. Mr Tash closed the door behind her and, for some reason best known to him, stood behind the coat stand. Half hidden, half visible. The minister stood in the middle of the room with a very false smile on his face, awaiting some kind of response from Zab. He quickly surveyed the room with its pictures of celebrities and other so-called important people. He tried to see where his own picture was but couldn't see one anywhere. The smile on his face disappeared.

Obviously, he thought, *this editor wasn't important enough to have a picture taken with this minister and that's why one wasn't being displayed in a very prominent place.*

He stopped looking. Turning back towards Zab, the false smile returned to his face. Zab hesitated for a moment. He wasn't used to getting visits from people that he thought more important than himself and the sight of Mr Tash trying to hide behind the coat stand somewhat threw him for a moment.

"Well, of course, I have time for you minister," replied Zab with a very changed attitude. He had recognised the minister from some of the many 'official meetings' that they had attended. Otherwise known as free parties to everyone else. He had also recognised Mr Tash, well half of him anyway, from the numerous encounters in the past where journalists had overstepped the mark and annoyed someone in the Great Council.

"Please sit down, won't you?" Zab said waving gently towards the two comfortable chairs on front of him with a very big equally as false smile on his face.

The minister thanked him and proceeded to sit down. He realised immediately that the chair was much lower than it should have been for he, too, had one just like it in his own office. Rather than sitting back and giving Zab the satisfaction, the minister sat forward taking a dominant position and counteracted the lowness of the chair. Mr Tash just stayed where he was, trying to pretend that Zab hadn't seen him walk in behind the minister. Stealth not being one of his better attributes. Not that he had any good attributes to talk of. Well, not any that most Smarians would consider as good anyway.

"And to what do I owe the pleasure, nay, honour of a visit from the Information minister himself?" grovelled Zab trying to impress the minister by knowing who he was and sucking up to him as was expected. As to the why he was there…Zab already knew!

"I believe that you are about to run a story which may well not be in the public's best interests," started the minister, "And one that, let's say, was acquired by not the most legal of ways."

Zab was about to object to that comment, all-be-it true, but was cut short by the minister with a raised hand as he continued.

"Now, I know that an editor with such an exemplary record as yourself wouldn't allow for this to happen. I know that even if there was a chance of a rogue journalist, shall we say, ever attempting to print in your newspaper a story that would harm the Great Council or the Great One himself, you would no doubt put a stop to it immediately. And...I have every faith in the belief that you wish to keep your paper's license to print!"

The minister was now almost halfway across Zab's huge desk. His fake smile now gone and replaced with a more threatening look. Zab had found himself pushing further and further back into his chair as the minister had menacingly crept towards him. The minister's false smile quickly came back to his face as he pulled back from the desk and sank back into his chair. His point being clearly made and received, he continued. "So! All I'm saying is that the documents that may or may not be in your or one of your journalist's possession, be returned forthwith to the Herald without anyone's knowledge of what happened. Indeed, not even the Herald himself be made aware that they were taken for any scandalous reason. Perhaps they might be returned to him by a paper that only had only the Smarian people's best interests at heart. A paper that was offered this information and paid for it only to preserve the freedom of the press and acknowledge the needs of its government to have certain 'restricted' information. Of course, then the Great Council might turn a blind eye to some of the newspaper's less savoury ways of obtaining stories about its undesirable characters in the entertainment world. They may even, hypothetically speaking of course, be able to furnish said newspaper with information of some juicy scandal that hasn't broken yet. Information which obviously wouldn't have come from any department within the Great Council." And with that the minister placed a folder on the desk marked *Top secret*.

Zab had thought about objecting citing freedom of the press, etc. but stopped himself with the sudden realisation that his words would fall on deaf ears. He sat back in his chair, resigned to the fact that Asil's story was never going to see the light of day. As to the offer of a story to replace it being placed on his desk, well, he would be foolish not to accept this very kind gesture. For the good of the Smarian people obviously! How exactly would he break the news to Asil was only a small insignificant detail. After all, he had lots of journalists, all waiting in the wings to impress him. He could afford to lose one even if they had been with the paper for a long time.

The minister could see that Zab was already way ahead of him and knew that the story was as good as dead. At least, this time!

"As for the journalist in question, Asil, I believe. Get her to report to my office sometime tomorrow as I have a very special story for her to cover. A story that only someone with her unique and obvious talents could best cover. A story that only a minister could give permission for anyone to cover. That should fool her, I mean, convince her to go along with our little agreement, don't you think? Good! Now perhaps." said the minister as he started to rise without waiting for a response.

"Perhaps we can be on our way now and say that the documents be back with the Herald by oh, what, say within the hour?"

Not waiting for a reply, he continued, "Good! I'm glad that we understand each other and look forward to hearing about his wretched celebrity and his nasty habit. Good day." And with that the minister walked out of Zab's office. He watched as the minister left and a very unhidden Mr Tash secreted himself out of the office. Convinced that no one had ever known he was there. Zab shook his head in despair and reached out for the folder ion his desk. He thumbed a few pages and then reached for the intercom.

"Get me Asil. Now!"

Back at the Great Chambers, the Herald had been looking everywhere for some documents that he had to relate to the Great One before lunch. He knew that he had put them in his briefcase when he had picked them up from the communications office yesterday afternoon before he had left for the day. He remembered that he had decided not to pass on the news to the Great One that evening as he would be accused of spoiling the Great One's appetite for dinner! He was baffled though as to why they weren't there now. He thought about where he had been and where and why he might have taken them out and put them down. He retraced his steps right up to the tragic and embarrassing moment in the bar with that really lovely journalist. Then it dawned on him. Perhaps he had mistakenly given her the important secret documents along with the poetry that she was so eager to print. Oh goodness! Could that possibly be the answer? Could he have inadvertently given that very nice journalist the wrong papers? He looked through his briefcase on more time. No, his poems weren't there and neither were the documents regarding the incident on Topside. Surely if he had, she would certainly have called him by now to return them? He remembered that she had said that she had "no interest in things like that!" there was only one thing for it. He would have to contact Asil and ask her.

Just as he was about to pick up the phone, there was a knock on his door and, without waiting for an answer, a messenger entered his small office. He was dressed in his

144

official bright yellow uniform that had obviously seen better days. A bit like the messenger himself really.

"Excuse me, mate? Are you what's known as the Herald?" enquired this somewhat scruffy looking individual.

"Yes I am," replied a rather indignant Herald.

"Well, I got a package for you," replied the messenger and held out a large envelope.

The Herald liked receiving packages and, just as he was about to take it, the messenger pulled it away quickly.

"Got to sign for it first, mate," demanded the messenger.

"But I don't know what it is yet," replied the Herald. "I might not want it!"

"Can't let you know what it is until you sign for it first." retorted the messenger. "You might not sign for it once you know what it is and then where would we be? I'd be standing here with no package and no signature. My boss would have a coronary if I went back to him without a package and no signature. Would sack me on the spot, he would. And me being a messenger for forty years and never once losing a package. More than my job's worth returning to base with no package and no signature. I have my reputation to think of you know!"

The messenger had stepped back from the Herald's desk and was clasping the package closely to his chest as though it was the most important thing in the world.

"Reputation! What reputation? You're just a messenger, not a member of the Great Council!" a very agitated Herald said. "Now give me my package!"

"What reputation?" continued the messenger moving the package further away as the Herald made a grab for it. "What reputation? I'll have you know that I've been messenger of the year for ten years almost on the run. There was only that one year when that no-good rookie won it. I know he only won it because he bribed the judges! I could have proved it as well if he'd not been promoted to the office. I could have been a contender for that office position, you know! Know the job back to front, I do. Better than those plebs that work in the office all day now. Never been out on the road seeing where the real work is done. No! My wife wouldn't speak to me for a week after I lost that year. Not such a bad thing to happen to me, I know, but that's not the point! Said she couldn't bear to speak to someone who could lose such a prestigious award! Even my kids got bullied at school because of it. The shame! No, so I made sure I won it back the following year. You see if I didn't!" retorted the messenger with much pride and emotion.

"That's all very well. Now if you would let me sign for the parcel, you could be on your way." replied the Herald trying a different tactic to get the parcel.

After a moment to think about what the Herald had just asked him, the messenger handed him a board with a piece of paper on it where it said *sign*. The Herald signed his name and handed the board back to the messenger, with his other hand ready to receive his parcel. With a big smile on his face and arms outstretched, he waited expectantly for his parcel. The messenger looked at the signature and then looked back at the Herald.

"Got any ID, have we, sir?" enquired the messenger.

"Got any ID? My name is on the door and the girl outside told you I was in here. What more do you need?" blurted out an exasperated Herald.

146

"Well, sir. Regulation 21, section 2, subsection 32a 'Proof of identity' states that I have to verify that, the person who signed for the parcel, is in fact, the person that they say they are. Can't leave a package without it, sir. Rules is rules!" stated the messenger standing bolt upright as if he was in the military.

"But I've signed for the damn thing. That's what you asked me to do! Now let me have the package!" and again the Herald made a lunge for it.

Too fast for the Herald, the messenger evaded the outstretched hands as the Herald leapt across the desk.

"ID first, sir. Them's the rules!" demanded a somewhat smug messenger.

"All right, all right," agreed the Herald finally giving in to the messenger's demands. "Anything to get that damn package." and he showed the messenger his pass for the Great Chambers.

"Could you take it out of the wallet please, sir? Could be a fake, you see." said the messenger peeking a glance at the pass.

"Remove the…Aaahhh!" exclaimed the Herald and hurriedly removed the pass from the wallet. His patience being tested to its limit by this job's worth of a messenger.

The messenger gave the pass a thorough examination. Turned it over to check both sides and gave more than a few glances backwards and forwards at the Herald and the photo on the pass.

Now convinced that he had indeed the right person, the messenger smiled and gave the Herald the package. He stepped back and with a salute and a "Have a nice day!" he turned and walked out the door.

The Herald was feeling a bit cranky after his brush with the messenger but was so relieved when he opened the package. For inside were the missing documents that he had been looking for. There was no card to say whom had returned the documents or indeed where they had been found just a note that said, "From a friend!" The Herald was just greatly relieved that they had been returned. He put them together with the other documents that he was taking to the Great One and left his office. As he walked towards the great Chamber, he allowed himself a smile and wondered whether he would see that nice young reporter again and when he could expect to see his poems in print.

Asil was to say a little mixed up. She was furious that her story was being pulled at the last moment. She had spent the entire day writing up her story and preparing herself for the fame that would surely follow only to find out that some bureaucrat had stopped it before it had ever been printed. She was furious that Zab had let her down. Taking some story about a clapped-out celebrity and his unusual habits over her story of the century. She had made a huge scene in Zab's office about it. The whole paper must have heard her rant on and on at Zab about loyalty to his reporters and to the paper!

Loyalty? Zab had thought. *Was there such a thing in journalism these days?*

Asil had continued on, not noticing he was thinking about something else, about how the people had the right to know what was going on. More so, how she now wouldn't get the recognition that she so desperately sought, deserved and needed! The only good thing to come out of it was that said bureaucrat had recognised her obvious talents and had requested her presence at the Great chambers for a job that only she could do! Her mind wasn't so much on what the job was, moreover, the implications of being asked directly by someone from the Great Council to do it whatever it was. It had been the only thing that had calmed her down. Zab had said how the minister himself had requested Asil be the one to cover this most influential story of a lifetime. How she had a duty to all Smarians to take the job, no matter what it was for the good of Smar itself. Zab had convinced her that she should put all other things aside to work with the Great Council as its first official reporter.

The first official reporter to the Great Council! Asil had thought. *Now that's a claim to fame! Just how important a person can the first official reporter be? Reporting directly to a minister of the Great Council! No one had ever held that title before and they had asked for it to be Asil over everyone else!* She continued with this train of thought whilst she copied all the documents that she had stolen from the Herald. She had been told to return them to the Herald by messenger that day but no one had said that she couldn't make copies first! Not that she didn't trust Zab or the minister. No, she didn't trust anyone!

Back at her desk, and with everyone whispering behind her back about what had transpired earlier that day, she was clearing up all the loose ends. A messenger had taken the original documents back to the Herald with strict instructions not to tell him where they had come from. Something that the messenger seemed only too pleased to do. Still with her mind on the impending fame and fortune of being the 'First official reporter to the Great Council', she was in the process of putting the copies she had made into her briefcase when she found the Herald's poems. She looked at them briefly before putting them very thoughtlessly on the edge of her desk.

"The things we do for a good story," she said to herself as she got up and left the paper for what was to be her last time. As she did so, she didn't notice or didn't care that as she got up she caused a slight breeze which lifted the Herald's poems off the edge of the desk. As they slowly slipped off the side of her desk, the Herald's dreams of seeing his beloved poems in print drifted perilously away as into the wastepaper bin they descended.

Chapter 12

The Rescue

The morning came far too quickly for some. They all knew what the rescue plan involved but few were confident that it was actually going to work. It seemed too simplistic. Unconvinced but with no other choice, they made their way to the landing site. All bar Tega and Nerak were more than a little apprehensive. Tega had to keep pulling Nerak back as she seemed to be the only one eager to get there and proceed with the rescue. Her lack of fear and contempt for the risks was not shared by the others. She was probably the only one with any confidence they might succeed! The rest held back. Putting off the rescue for as long as they possibly could. Even the ever positive Krun had his doubts. Tega, Ha'an and Nerak reached the top of the hill first. They laid down so as not to be seen and pointed their binoculars towards the landing site. The camp was much as it had been yesterday. The bubble machine was still parked out in front of the main structure and was silent. The morning sun glistening off a huge shiny array of mirror-like flat pieces laid facing in its direction and a couple more on the top of that monstrous machine. Nothing moving. All three searched for signs of Woc but could see none. Tega pointed to the smaller domed structure where he thought the scorse would be held.

"What makes you think that's where the scorse is?" asked Ha'an still surveying the landing site for any signs of movement.

"Well…that's where they take anything they find first so it's the most likely place for them to hold it," explained Tega. He purposefully didn't tell them that he had also seen them smash whatever they found with a large hammer and chisel and take the smaller parts into the larger dome. He assumed to examine them further. Something that they hadn't done to the scorse!

"Why there? Why not further inside the structure where those green things are that they seem to take great care over?" enquired Nerak now looking at said dome through her binoculars.

Tega hesitated. Should he tell them now what he has seen or should he leave it until later? He decided to avoid telling them now in case they thought him mad. Even he had trouble with what he saw so how could he expect anyone else to believe him? No, let them find out later if they had to at all. He hoped that the machines would be away long enough for them not to have to find out but there was always the chance that they could come back. Catching them in their attempt of rescuing the scorse and before they had got away.

"Because that's where they seem to examine all the samples. Only the machines themselves go further in to remove their…" he stopped himself there.

"To remove their what?" asked both Ha'an and Nerak now staring at Tega quizzically.

"To…to…oh, you'll see when we get there. We haven't got time for tittle tattle now." replied Tega anxious to change the subject and fortunately for him something happened that did change the subject very quickly.

For out of the main dome emerged the two walking machines. Ha'an and Nerak quickly put their binoculars back to their eyes and watched what was going on, much to the relief of Tega. He breathed a sigh and then he, too, began to watch the machines. To await their chance for their daring rescue attempt.

Dez was sitting on the floor further down the hill in a bit of a dilemma again. Whilst he had been the one to say that they must go and retrieve Woc, he had hoped that it was going to be the others and not him as well. As much as he loved Woc and was more than grateful to him for saving his life twice, he really didn't think that he would have to do the same in return. However, he was there now and just had to hope upon hope that Tega and Ha'an's plan would work. His parents had said that the army would make a real Smarian of him. He hadn't realised that it would be so quickly into his national service though! Yes, perhaps after the first six, no eight, nine or even ten months in but not in his first two weeks! Then he thought about Woc and how he had befriended Dez when most people would just mock him. Woc may be just a stupid animal used for purely powering their equipment to most but to Dez, he had become a true friend and companion. Someone who never judged Dez for all his faults and failings. Something that was rare for Dez as even his own parents and family thought him more than a bit dim. All through his life, he had been put down by everyone. At school, he had no real friends, just a few scared kids that were as bullied as much as he was. Kids that kept each other company and stuck together when they weren't being bullied. Unfortunately, as soon as one of them got picked on the others, instead of banding together for strength, would disperse in all directions. Grateful that it wasn't their turn. Even the teachers had called him useless and made him feel inadequate. He was told in no short terms that he would amount to nothing as he never tried hard enough at anything. Giving up in the first hurdle. Lacking in confidence to work past it. Mind you, no one ever helped him believe that he could achieve anything either. All taking the easier path of watching him fail and criticising him for it. The two saving graces from this whole mission was his friendship with Woc and the fact that Krun had told him that, as he seemed to enjoy it so much, his parent would give him a job on their ranch in the east tending the scorse as soon as he had completed his national service. So saving Woc was now something that he had to do. For the friend in need of rescue, a job in the east and more importantly for his own self-esteem!

Karel and Krun were behind Dez, unaware of the thoughts and dilemmas that he was trying to deal with. Krun hadn't said much all trip. Whilst he had always tried to look on the bright side and smile, this trip had really tested his resolve. After every negative event on Topside (And there had been a few. Being 'volunteered' for this mission, the storm, losing Dez and the scorse, the mountain and now these fiendishly strange and dangerous machines!), he had always tried to find a positive from the outcome. Easier said than done and sometimes much to the annoyance of the others. Being positive in the relative safety of Below was infinitely easier than the uncertain, dangerous surroundings and the events of Topside but he tried his best. His laid-back happy attitude had sometimes made the others wonder about his sanity. Still at least he didn't have to put up with the herds of scorse as he had to at home. One he could cope with but being trapped at Below with hundreds of them was sometimes a bit too much for ones nostrils! They may have been in the wide and open caverns of the east and he had become accustomed to the smell of the scorse but come mating season! Well, that was when all but a few of the older scorse filled the moss-covered fields. All gorging themselves on its rich foliage. That and the act of mating itself all culminated in them doing what came naturally in a very, very excessive way. Filling the air and almost pressurising the caverns. The concentration of the gas during this short period of time not allowing for any fires for obvious reasons. Let's just say that, with their eyes and nostrils now streaming from the horrendous smell, Krun and the other poor unfortunate souls that lived there more than welcomed the opening of the enormous hatches. Celebrated at the release of the build-up of this excessively large amount of the obnoxious gas. Thank goodness, it was for only one month of the year! Hence, why Krun thought Topside a breath of fresh air.

Karel had spent most of his time admiring the sky and basking in the wide-open space of Topside. The others had commented on the fact that he had less questions and a smile on his face whilst out in the open and a frown on his face and an abundance of questions when they had been inside the mountain. The questions being part of his coping mechanism for his fear of being enclosed anywhere but they didn't know that. Ha'an had joked that perhaps Karel preferred outside to inside! This made them all laugh and Karel had joined in whilst secretly wanting to shout out that he did indeed prefer being Topside as opposed to anywhere like Below or inside a mountain. The others would have certainly thought that there was something wrong with him if he had so he just played along with them. Karel looked at Krun and was amazed to see that Krun had nodded off.

"Krun!" whispered Karel as loudly as he dared nudging Krun as he did.

"Um. What?" replied Krun without moving a muscle.

"How can you sleep at a time like this? Aren't you the least bit worried about what we are about to do?" asked Karel somewhat astounded that anyone could sleep this close to the landing site and those frightening machines.

"What's to worry about? We haven't done anything yet," replied Krun still not moving.

"But we're about to go into the landing site of these machines and attempt to rescue our scorse. Doesn't that worry you at least a little bit?" questioned Karel.

Krun breathed a sigh, opened his eyes and turned to Karel. He had been perfectly happy waiting for things to happen without making a noise but now found that he had to explain himself. Something that he never liked doing much.

"Go with the flow, Smarian!" was generally his motto. Krun was so laid back that if he was indeed any more laid back, he'd fall over. Tail or no tail!

"It's like this," he started. "At the moment, we are just sitting here, yeah?"

Karel nodded a reluctant nervous acceptance of his comment.

"What we have to do, we have to do! Can't change that so why worry about it? It's not like I can change the fact that the stupid scorse got captured, can I? No! I can't change the fact that we really need it to get back to base, can I?"

Again Karel nodded reluctantly.

"Well, no but…"

"No! It just happened and I have to deal with it. All I can do is exactly what gets asked of me and hope that it works. What I can do is be positive about it and make sure that whatever happens, I do what I can to influence the outcome for the better. None of that negative crap that's going on inside of his head right now." said Krun pointing at Dez. "I look at what's happened as a positive."

"How so?" queried Karel. Puzzled by his remark.

"If the scorse hadn't have been captured, we would be just looking at this strange camp from a distance. Now I get the chance to see it up close like no one else ever will. I get the opportunity to see something and do something that no one else has ever done. Now that's got to be a good thing, hasn't it?"

Karel wasn't convinced but before he could say anything, Krun continued, "Why would I spend my time worrying about something that may or may not happen? If I worried about everything that could go wrong, I wouldn't do anything. I'd be so hung up on the negative things in life that I wouldn't be able to see or enjoy the positive side of life and all it has to offer. Granted, being here wouldn't be my first choice but whilst I'm stuck here, I'm damn well going to make the best of it. Hell, when was the last time you got to go on a rescue mission? Never! And you may never get the chance to either. Yeah, I know that this mission could have negative consequences but, who knows, we may actually pull it off! So, stop worrying about what might happen and live for what is actually happening. Think positively and things will be positive! You might just enjoy life a whole lot more!"

Karel looked a bit confused but Krun just laid back down.

"Give me a nudge when something starts to happen." And with that, Krun rolled over, closed his eyes and went back to sleep.

Karel tried to think of something to say nut for every question that he came up with, he thought of what Krun had said and somehow he made a strange kind of sense. It may not have changed their situation but it did change the way Karel thought about it and kept his mind on something positive rather than the danger that they might face.

Athan was at the back because of his size as usual. By now though, he realised that his size was something that he could be proud of and rejoice in and not something to be ashamed of. After his little scare inside the mountain and being made to go into the dark to see what was there, he had a new confidence. Nerak had commented with great respect and admiration for his enormous physique. How she had been amazed that he didn't see it that way and convinced him to take a leaf out of Krun's book and be more positive about his build. Something that he had thought long and hard over. No longer would he cower down and try to make himself look smaller. No more would he try and hide in a corner away from people so as not to scare them with his bulk. Now he knew it was okay to be big and different and he knew that he could help his new friends because of it. He no longer walked with a whimper. He stood tall and proud! Being 'volunteered' for this mission was probably one of the best things that had ever happened to him, even though he didn't think it at the time. He had made friends and had gained an immense amount of confidence in himself. Positivity! Perhaps being around the ever positive Krun had rubbed off after all. He certainly was no longer the sad Smarian he had been before he got here. Athan smiled to himself. Finally he was happy and content with his lot. Just the rescue to pull off now!

Nothing happened for ages. Was this going to be the day that none of the machines left the main domes? Would they have to wait another day for their chance to mount the rescue? The three of them remained silent. Constantly surveying the landing site for any sign of activity. Eventually their patience paid off and the two machines had emerged from the structure. They did their usual check of all the surrounding objects. To what end, no one knew. Slowly walking around from one to another. Stopping to look at them for a brief moment and then moving on to the next one. Then there was a change to their daily routine. This time things were different. After they had checked everything as usual, they began collecting all the smaller items that were scattered around the landing site. Picking them up and putting them back into the object that they had landed in. Even the items that they checked every day were being removed and place inside the landing object. Non-stop they worked. Continually back and forth until only the main domed structures, the smaller dome, the shiny mirrors and the big upside-down dome remained. Everything had been put away meticulously well. Some of the samples of rocks that they had collected were also taken from the small dome and stored aboard the landing object. They had worked without stopping for well over two hours before re-entering the main dome. Tega had watched closely to see if the scorse was amongst the things being loaded up but was pleased to see that it wasn't. That would have scuppered any rescue attempt! After an hour or so, the machines reappeared from the main dome and this time climbed inside the bubble machine. With a whining noise and a huge duct cloud, they sped off out and away from the landing site.

Tega watched as they disappeared into the distance leaving a trail of red dust behind them. Now was their chance!

With the machines now well out of view, Tega and the others made their way as quickly as possible towards the smaller dome. They kept looking around all the time as they went towards the dome just in case the machines unexpectedly turned around and came back. As they approached the dome, they all began to slow down. From a distance, the dome had looked quite solid but as they approached they could see that it was moving slowly. Its many panels that made up the dome seemed to move with the wind in and out. Its slow motion giving the impression that it was breathing. Breathing in time with the environment as if they were one. Could it be possible that this 'structure' was actually alive? Tega realised that they had all stopped in the middle of the landing site and immediately hit the deck. Everyone else did the same, not knowing exactly why but all thought it best. Nothing stirred. The dome continued to 'breathe' but nothing else moved. Tega got up and waved everyone on towards the dome cautiously. There were a few bemused looks as to why they had stopped in the first place but all thought it a good idea to keep moving. Athan picked Dez up as he passed him. Dez had buried his head so far into the ground that he hadn't noticed that everyone else had moved off.

"Come on," said Athan. "You can stick with me at the back."

"Thanks!" said Dez as he followed behind the bulk of Athan occasionally having to glance around him to see where they were going.

They all made it to the entrance of the smaller dome. Smaller dome! It was enormous. Its door was larger than the entrance to the caves in the mountain! Fortunately it was ajar and Ha'an and Tega, who were at the front, peered into the vast void of the dome. Nerak was examining the walls of the dome. Although from a distance it had looked metallic and solid, she was surprised to find that in fact it was quite pliable. It looked like metal and was quite thick but moved like a heavy cloth. She drew her knife from its holster and just as she was about to plunge it into the wall to get a sample, Tega grabbed her hand. She looked at him. Furious that he had stopped her.

"Let's concentrate on the task at hand first, shall we?" he said quietly but very firmly. "Besides which you have no idea what might happen if you cut into its walls."

Nerak reluctantly put her knife back in its holster. She wasn't used to being told what to do but realised that this was an unusual place to be and perhaps caution was, in this case, a better idea.

Tega moved back to the open door and peered in once again. Inside there were all kinds of boxes and containers with the strange markings all over them surrounding the walls. Some of the boxes had flashing lights and what looked like cables hanging from them. In the centre was a massive table with all manner of shiny objects scattered around its top and in the middle was a glass container. Tega stood on his tiptoes as if to try and see more. He could just about make out that within the container was their scorse! He was curled up in a corner of the container, not moving.

"I can see the scorse!" whispered Tega to Ha'an who passed the message down the line.

Dez was relieved to hear the news that his beloved Woc was there but had to ask the question rather louder than he ought to.

"Is he alive?"

Everyone turned to Dez and shushed him almost as loud as he had spoken, then all turned back to Tega for the answer. All waiting hopefully for good news. Tega tuned back to the container and now looked though his binoculars at the scorse. There was no sign of movement. He was just about to say something when Woc's head rose up, looked around and, thinking that he was still all alone inside his transparent prison, put his head down again almost as if in tears.

"Yes. It's alive!" reported Tega.

Everyone was relieved for a moment, especially Dez. Then it dawned on them that they would now have to rescue the damn thing. Tega and Ha'an immediately huddled together to discuss how they were going to get to the top of the table when Nerak tried to butt in.

"Excuse me," she started. "Why don't you just…"

She was cut short by one of Tega's hands being placed over her mouth. Something that really annoyed her. Annoyed wasn't really the correct word but it was the politest!

"When we want your help, we'll ask for it! At the moment, we are weighing up our options and we will inform you of what we will be doing as soon as we know. Now, please move away." replied Tega and turned back to Ha'an.

Ha'an said nothing. He wasn't about to argue with either of them.

"But," Nerak tried again only to have the hand replaced.

"Go away!" barked Tega and turned back to Ha'an yet again.

Nerak muttered something very unladylike under her breath and walked back to the others. Tega and Ha'an were still huddled together, deep in conversation about how they would attempt the rescue. Shall they do it this way or send someone to do it that way when Krun tapped them on the shoulder.

"What is it?" demanded Tega angrily turning around to Krun. He'd had enough of being interrupted.

"Yes!" joined in Ha'an not wishing to be outdone in the chain of command. "What is it?"

Krun didn't say anything, merely pointed at Nerak as she was now halfway up one of the table legs with a rope dangling behind her. Both Tega and Ha'an's jaws dropped.

"She said to wait until she was halfway up before telling you what she was doing. She said…" emphasis on the she! "…as you weren't going to listen to her, she was just going to do it anyway. Then Athan piped up that, as he was the biggest, he would go with her to help and protect her."

Tega and Ha'an looked just below Nerak to see Athan climbing right behind her. After a short stunned silence, Tega shouted up to Nerak,

"Are you mad? What are you going to do when you get up there? Have you thought about that?" he demanded without realising that he was actually shouting.

"Not really," she replied stopping for a moment whilst waiting for Athan to catch up. "Just thought that I would do something rather than twitter on about doing nothing. I'll think of something when I get up there. Look and see what the situation is and get back to you."

And with that she continued climbing. Athan looked down at them, which wasn't the brightest of things to do as he hated heights, wished he hadn't, smiled nervously and continued on after Nerak.

Tega and Ha'an looked at each other and then back at the table. There was nothing that they could do about it now. All they could do was move closer to the table to wait and see what happened next.

"Of all the stupid things to do! That stubborn, over-educated, frustrating, arrogant, over-confident female had to go and do that!" ranted a very irate Tega.

Ha'an placed a hand on Tega's shoulder and said, "I know. I like her too!"

Nerak reached the top and elegantly swung up and stood at the table's edge. She watched as Athan completed the final few feet. Athan wasn't far behind her but was far from elegant with his swing onto the top. After several failed attempt and eventually with help from Nerak, he scrambled onto the top of the table. He laid there for a minute until, relieved that he had finally made it, he got up and stood next to Nerak. Both had huge grins on their faces. First part done! They waved at the others below, who sighed with relief.

"Now to get that scorse," Nerak said to Athan with an excited smile on her face. She was loving every moment of this!

They looked across the crowded table towards the glass container and started to make their way to it. Carefully avoiding all the strange objects that blocked their path. The table was strewn with all manner of weird objects. Some looked like extremely sharp cutting tools. Other like huge clamps whilst others were just... well, weird! Some had flashing lights and some made buzzing noises. From up there they could also see that all around the dome were other large cabinet structures with hundreds of flashing lights and dials similar but much more complex and sophisticated to their own radio. Were these the machines way of communicating from whence they came? Were they the same as the walking machines but unable to move? Could they see or hear them?

Whatever their use was anyone's guess. Nerak and Athan, as quickly as they could, made their way across the table to the big glass container that imprisoned the scorse. Nerak arrived first, of course, and looked at the scorse. It wasn't moving at all. Nerak banged on the glass wall. Nothing! She tried again. Harder this time. Still the scorse didn't move. As she was about to strike the glass for the third time, Athan stopped her, smiled and hit the glass with his mighty hands. Moving the container slightly. Woc looked up somewhat bewildered expecting to see his tormentors staring down at him again. He wondered with what they were going to poke him with this time and how much would it hurt. Whether they would again restrain him with their huge hands and try to puncture his tough skin again with their sharp needles. He looked up to the top of the container but saw nothing. As he was about to lay back down again thinking that nature was just playing a cruel trick, Athan hit the glass again. This time Woc looked up and straight into the eyes of Nerak. She smiled with relief and said something but Woc couldn't hear or understand it. He didn't care though as it was a friendly face that he recognised. With this, Woc began to run around excitedly wondering what was going to happen next. Now that she knew that the scorse was okay, Nerak thought about how to get it out of the container. It didn't take long before she tied the rope around her waist and, with Athan standing at his full height against the glass, she started climbing up Athan. Once she reached his shoulders, he lifted her up by her feet so that she could almost reach the top of the container.

"Almost there! Just a few inches more!" Nerak urged Athan on.

Athan pushed up a little further, reaching up as far as he could go as Nerak managed to grip the top and slowly pull herself up the rest of the way. She again elegantly swung herself over the top of the container and straddled the edge of the glass wall. Athan grabbed one end of the rope and tied it around his substantial waist. The other he threw up to Nerak and she, too, tied it around her waist. With that done, Nerak gently slipped over the side of the container and Athan slowly lowered her to the floor. Woc was so excited to see them he did what came naturally and farted! Nerak almost passed out from the smell of the overexcited scorse. She untied herself and managed to get the rope around Woc before she did. His obnoxious stench sticking in her nose and mouth.

"You are one smelly scorse!" she proclaimed as she patted his head.

With one hand holding her nose and mouth shut, she beckoned to Athan to start pulling the scorse up. Athan nodded his understanding but as he did, there was an almighty thud. Everyone, up top and below, stopped and looked towards the door of the dome. Slowly the door began to creak open. Nerak beckoned with more urgency for Athan to lift the scorse. Banging on the glass to try and get his attention but

Athan's eyes were transfixed on the opening door. It swung fully open and there in the doorway stood a huge walking machine exactly like the others.

Another one? thought Tega. *How can there be another one?*

He had only ever seen the machines two at a time. It had never entered his head that they might not have been the same ones! Now there was a huge machine about to walk in on their rescue attempt. This certainly wasn't in any of their plans! What do they do now?

The machine surveyed the room and looked at the table straight at the three of them. It seemed somewhat startled at first but then started to move towards the table. Nerak continued shouting and banging on the glass for Athan to pull. No need for stealth now but Athan's eyes were still riveted on the machine now heading their way. As it drew closer, they could finally see into the huge bulbous head of the machine. They were now in awe at what they saw. For instead of some mechanical machine, they saw a face! Not a Smarian type of face but a face anyway. The face was lit by lights all around the glass bowl and they could see its features very clearly. It had two eyes, a nose, mouth and was a pinky kind of colour. A monstrous living being was inside the machine! It must have been female as well as it had short yellow hair on its head. Its mouth was moving as if trying to say something but no sound emerged from it. Probably because the huge glass bowl that this face was surrounded by was preventing any noise from coming out of it. Nerak had stopped banging and shouting at Athan. She, too, was transfixed on the face inside the machine as it closed in. Both hypnotised by this creature's well-lit features inside the glass bowl. Only Woc seemed aware of the danger that they were in. He had already seen the faces in the machines and knew what they had done to him, they would probably do to the others if caught. There was only one thing for it. He had to get the attention of Nerak and he only knew of one way to do that. Yes! He farted! Farted for all he was worth! It worked! Nerak pulled a horrible face as she gagged on the enormous amount of the obnoxious gas that this little scorse had conjured up. A bit like giving someone smelling salts to bring them to! It did the trick though as she immediately came to her senses. She banged on the glass again at Athan trying to get his attention and finally she did. Athan shook as he, too, came back to reality and turned and looked at Nerak.

"Pull!" she shouted at the top of her voice. There was definitely no need to be quiet now! But the machine was nearly upon them and just as its outstretched arm was about to reach out and grab Athan, it pulled away. Not waiting to see why, Nerak again shouted at Athan to pull the scorse up.

"No!" screamed Athan his attention now back on the task at hand. "Jump on his back and I'll pull you both up together."

"You can't lift both of us," pleaded Nerak looking back at the machine and wondering why it had stopped and was now clumsily turning around and looking elsewhere.

"I'm not leaving you! I can do it! Get on the scorse's back now! Please!" pleaded a determined Athan.

Nerak took one last look at the machine as it moved away, looked into Athan's eyes and leapt onto the scorse's back. Woc was somewhat taken aback. He had never had anyone jump onto his back before. But then again, he had never been abducted by strange monster machines and experimented on either so he just put up with it. It really was a strange day!

Athan had to use all of his considerable strength to pull them up. Just lifting the scorse would have been a hard-enough challenge but with the added weight of Nerak, it was almost impossible. Every muscle in his body was crying out in pain. He wanted to give up. To let go and hide in a corner until it was over but he knew that he couldn't. That would have been the old him and he wasn't about to go back to being that person again. He looked deep within himself and found the strength to go on. Nerak shouting her encouragement all the way as he pulled with every ounce of strength that he could find. His body ached with every inch that he pulled them up. His blood boiling up and his muscles bulging with the intense effort. A voice inside of him was telling him to keep pulling. To keep going even though he wanted to quit and he did keep going. He screamed out in pain as it felt like his four arms would wrench themselves out of their sockets at any moment. As they neared the top, Nerak jumped up and pulled herself to the top of the container and straddled the top again. Athan was slightly relieved that some of the weight had gone but was still holding on and pulling. Nerak tried as best she could to help the scorse over the top but it wouldn't go. Its wormlike body and all those legs hindering every attempt to get it over the top. So, without thinking it through properly, she pushed the scorse over the edge. First its top half and then, very quickly, the rest followed in a rush. Unfortunately, Athan hadn't realised that they were at the top as he had his eyes shut and was still pulling. A brief moment of relief as his body could feel no weight and that he didn't have to pull any more. A brief moment indeed as when he opened his eyes, all he could see was the scorse hurtling down the side of the container at him at speed and unceremoniously landing directly on top of him knocking them both to the floor. Nerak slid down the side of the container and landed on the table hard. She winced with the pain of dropping from such a height but wasted no time in checking on Athan and the scorse. Athan was a bit dazed but got up. The scorse, his landing being softened by Athan, was none the worse from his ordeal but daren't leave their side. All three of them made their way to the edge of the table as quick as they dare. Dodging the strange instruments as they went. As they got to the edge and looked down, they could see why the being in the machine had stopped and moved away. For below them and running all over the floor were their compatriots. A very bemused and cumbersome machine being was trying to grab at them but to no avail. Twisting and turning as best it could, to catch something. Anything! They ran at the machine to gain its attention and then ran behind all the boxes and object littering the floor of the dome once it turned towards them. The being inside this machine was far too slow to catch them but was trying its absolute best. As soon as one looked like he was getting cornered, another ran at the machine to distract it. Waving their arms around and throwing whatever they could lay their hands on at this beast in a machine. Hitting it as hard as they could to keep it occupied whilst the other escaped. Every time taking care not to get squashed by the monster's huge feet. It was almost comic! Again and again, they did this to keep the thing away from the table. Each randomly helping out the other. Sometimes all at once. Sometimes running into each other as they were looking the other way. At one point, the machine being looked so disorientated that they thought it might fall over as it stumbled and fought to stay upright. Its backpack hitting all the surrounding items and knocking them over. Supplying more ammunition for our motley crew to throw at it. Another thing that our gallant crew had to avoid for fear of being crushed beneath them as they fell.

Nerak and Athan wasted no time in securing the rope to a heavy object on the table. The other end still being attached to the scorse. They pushed a very reluctant scorse to the edge where it had concertinaed itself up to stop it from going over the edge. Athan and Nerak looked at each other, smiled, raised a boot and encouraged the scorse off the edge. Encouraged? Unceremoniously kicked it off really as they had no time lose. Woc had closed his eyes as he went over the edge. He briefly wondered why his friends that had bothered rescuing him were now trying to kill him by kicking him off the table! It wasn't until the rope bit and he found himself dangling in the air, did he realise that he wasn't actually falling to his doom. He looked down and then decided against it and closed his eyes. It was a long drop!

They lowered him to the ground where a grateful Dez was waiting to collect him. Dez had thought himself too slow to join in the frolics the others were indulging in. Too slow and petrified as well! As the scorse hit the ground, Dez threw his arms around him and gave him a big hug. The fact that the scorse had been farting all the way down in fear didn't bother Dez. He had his friend back! Nerak and Athan came down the table leg much quicker than they went up. They only stopped once when the huge machine being bumped into it whilst chasing the others nearly knocking them both clean off the rope. Bouncing them precariously off the side of the table and swinging them around and around. Crashing them back into the table again and again until it stopped. Both praying that the rope stay secure to the object holding it at the top. Once on the ground, the four of them waited for their chance and made their way towards the entrance. Dodging the machine being, the others as they ran their chaotic random paths and the objects being thrown and landing in all directions. Pandemonium had broken loose. Everyone screaming and shouting at the tops of their voices with fear as well as trying to distract the being. Mainly with fear though and rightly so! Having seen Nerak, Athan, Dez and Woc making for the entrance, they, too, had started their way back in that direction. The only problem was that the machine being was now following them as well. Athan had stopped and was now waving them onto the entrance and they didn't need telling twice. They all made it to the entrance at a speed most of them didn't even know they could reach. Not one of them taking a moment to look back. They already knew that the machine being was right behind them…and closing! Just one of its clumsy, slow steps was equal to about ten of theirs so speed was of the essence! The machine being was too close for comfort. As the last one shot out of the dome, Athan managed to push over two large containers he had found by the entrance tripping the machine being up. Arms and legs going in every direction trying to maintain its balance as it fell with no grace at all. Grabbing at thin air as it fell. Finally bouncing off the floor with a large thud, it now laid still for the briefest of moments. Then, pushing up with its arms as it struggled to get to its knees. Taking several attempts to push itself up. The weight of its own backpack making it difficult to balance and move. Eventually it grabbed at a door handle and pulled itself up to its knees. It took a few moments to steady itself before it could look around to see what had happened. The floor of the dome was strewn with the wreckage of the preceding chaos but not one of our band of brave Smarians were to be seen. By then, they had all disappeared. The machine being rose to its feet and surveyed its surroundings. Picking up each item as if looking to see if what had thrown it was till hiding somewhere. After a while and realising that it was now alone, it walked around for a bit and then went back to the main structure. They had made it!

Chapter 13

Safe but What Now?

The race to get as far away as possible was on! Everyone wanting to be the first! None wanting to be last. To be last was to be the first one that the machine being could possibly catch. The lead had changed many times on the way over to the relative safety of the rocks. There had been no thought to sex or rank in his race. Merely to get away from that menacing machine. Nerak had been surprised at how fast Dez and the scorse had been as they barged past her without any dignity in a bid to get as far away as possible from the dome and the machine being. All three had been passed by a stampeding Athan which no one wanted to get in the way of. His huge bulk showing no mercy to anyone or anything in his way. Jumping over rocks that most would run around, he bounded his way to the front. Breaking his stride for no one and no thing. Even the laid back Krun was trying his hardest to be first. Keeping pace with the long legs of Karel as they sped away from the mayhem of the dome. Tega and Ha'an had tried to shout that everyone should stay behind them but no one listened as they passed them at great speed. They were far too intent on getting away rather than listen to someone trying to bark out orders especially if it put them at the back. No one stopped running until they had reached the safety of the rocks at the edge of the landing site. Once there they dived, literally in some cases, behind the rocks for cover trying to catch their breath. It was only then that Tega had taken a moment to look back and see if the machine being was still chasing them. Nope! No sign of anything chasing them. Athan had put paid to that with his heroic toppling of the machine being. Tega sat back and sighed with relief. He looked around at this motley crew. Ha'an was on his back holding his chest as if to try and stop his racing heart from trying to escape. Nerak was sitting back and laughing. She had actually enjoyed the rescue mission even if it didn't go quite as any of them had anticipated. Karel was again looking up to the sky with a smile on his face. He turned to Krun who was sitting beside him and patted him on the back. Krun just looked at him and smiled back.

"See what can happen if you think positive thoughts." smiled Krun and they both started to laugh.

Athan was flat out on his back mumbling "Thank you, thank you!" to the sky. A religious Smarian by no means but like most, when the odds were against him, would ask for, accept and give thanks for help from any entity going regardless of belief! He may have been the biggest and the fastest of all of them but he had screamed like a small child all the way from the structure to the rocks.

Dez was gasping for breath and hugging Woc at the same time. He was trying not to think about what had just happened as it scared him half to death. Woc, on the other hand, seemed unmoved by what had happened and was sniffing Dez's backpack for something to eat. All that had passed the last couple of days were now of no consequence to Woc. Food was now his priority.

After a while they all got up and moved back to where they had camped the night before. Th sky began to darken as night fell on this day of days. Each erected their tent and sat down by the campfire to eat. No one had said much all evening. Each reflecting on the day's events with their own thoughts and feelings. It was Athan who spoke first.

"What were those things?" he started. "I never thought for once that there would actually be something alive inside those machines. Do you think that it means that those other machines had living things inside them too?"

"Yes." joined in Karel. "And where do you think they came from? Certainly not from Smar! If anything like that existed on Smar, we would know about it, wouldn't we? And if they don't come from Smar…well where do they come from?"

Ha'an looked up from his plate. He looked around at them all and said, "Well, when I was on the last mission to watch the last machine, there was certainly nothing inside it. They may have looked like they came from the same place but the machine I saw then was nowhere as big as that one. Nor did it build other domes and things. It simply roamed over Topside as if it was looking for something. The Great Council had told us to follow it and see what it did and where it went. To capture it if we could and this we attempted. All our attempts to stop it or communicate with it were fruitless. We could even wander right up to it and it wouldn't see us or attempt to do anything. Very unlike that machine being today. We tried to stop it by blocking its path and many were killed. It just continued on its way without any compassion for the

Smarians that it crushed. It was like it didn't even know we existed. Those that it didn't crush to death there and then died later from their injuries. I was the only one that survived. Part of the plan to capture it was that I climbed aboard. Opened it up I did but only found a lot of brightly coloured cables leading off to who knows where. I only managed to get off it when it fell into a deep gulley and it couldn't get out. The Great council were contacted once I got back to base and they sent out a special team who took over and told me to leave it to them and never talk of it again. I never thought that I would be out here again running for my life from such things."

"What happened to that machine?" enquired Nerak very interested in its whereabouts.

"Don't know," replied Ha'an. "I was never told and was led to believe that it was that I never asked if you know what I mean. Rumours said that it was taken somewhere. Somewhere to be studied away from the prying eyes of the general public. It was only when I got very drunk and told a reporter what I saw that I heard from the Great Council again and here I am."

"Well, what do we do now?" asked Karel.

Just as Tega was about to say something, there was an enormous explosion. The ground began to shake and everyone thought that the bubble machine was upon them again. They looked around in all directions wondering whether to run and hide or just sit here and wait for the machine to show itself. Resigned to their fate. But it didn't show itself. The noise continued and the ground still shook but nothing came their way. Confused they continued to look around until Krun cried out. "Look!"

He was pointing up at the night sky. For there, rising quickly upwards was what looked like the object that the machine beings had arrived in. They were all looking up to see a bright red glow of flames shooting from the belly of the object as it raced into the night sky. Picking up speed as it reached higher and higher. No one said anything. All were in a stunned silence as they watched this ball of flames disappear into the night sky. Moving higher and higher until it became nothing more than a bright spot amongst the stars. The thunderous noise had subsided and Topside became silent once more. It was Tega who broke the silence.

"They've left! Gone!" he cried.

Everyone looked at him a bit puzzled. Left? What did he mean?

"The machines or whatever they were. They've gone!"

Everyone still looked at him very confused.

"That bright ball in the sky. It was them. I saw the exact same thing the day they arrived. It's them, I tell you. They've gone!"

Everyone began to look at each still in a stunned silence when they were suddenly amazed to see that Tega had got up and was now doing a jig around the campfire. Laughing as he danced. The confused silence continued with glances of disbelief going between them until Dez began to laugh. So did Karel and pretty soon, they were all laughing. Nerak got up and joined Tega in his jig, laughing all the way and was joined by all but Ha'an. He sat not laughing and looking at the floor. Everyone else was having far too good a time to pay much attention. The relief of the machine things leaving overcoming all their emotions. Eventually Nerak came and sat beside Ha'an as the others continued to party. Relieved that they were finally out of danger.

"What's the matter Ha'an? They've gone! It's over! Why aren't you joining in the celebrations?"

Ha'an didn't look up from the floor. His mind was far from a partying mood. He sighed and then looked straight into Nerak's eyes.

"It's not over, is it?" he replied. "They'll be back, won't they? They found the scorse and saw us as we rescued it. They know we're here now. They'll be back!"

Nerak sighed. The kind of sigh that said she understood. The kind of sigh that knew exactly what he meant.

"Yes, you're probably right. They will be back. But next time, it will be different. Next time we will know what to expect. Next time we will know that they are alive and not just machines. Next time we will be ready for them. To find out who they are and where they come from. To find out why they've come here and perhaps find out what's out there!" she said pointing at the vastness of the night sky with all its bright lights twinkling away and trying to comfort him.

"And what if they're hostile? What if they've come here to enslave us and take away our way of life? What if next time there are hundreds of them? What if…"

Nerak had put her hand over his mouth to stop him. She could see how upset he was and where he was coming from.

"So many negative thoughts." she smiled. "Don't let Krun hear you talking that way. He'd have you listening to him all night about the positive side of life."

Ha'an gave a slight grin. She was right! Krun would spend all night talking to him about the virtues of positive thinking! Nerak continued.

"We have no idea about what is going to happen in the future. It's just part of the beauty of the journey of life. All we can do is live for today and the moment. Yes, there is the possibility that they may be hostile but that equally leaves open the possibility that they might not be! After all, they must have travelled a long way to get here. They obviously have technology well beyond ours. I would like to think that because of that they are also more enlightened with higher morals. That violence and hostility is something that they have gone beyond in their quest for knowledge. To know that neither bring peace and tranquillity. Either way, they've gone for now and I, for one, am grateful for that. Now, get up and dance with us. Celebrate this day and our successful rescue and escape. For tomorrow's another day and another adventure!"

Nerak got up and, her smile beaming, was extending her arms out to Ha'an. Ha'an didn't budge. Nerak held her arms out again and stamped her foot. Ha'an grinned. She really was a forceful young lady! He got up and took her hands and both went and joined in the festivities. To hell with the "what ifs?" as they celebrated the here and now.

Unseen and observing from a distance as always were four lights. Three small ones and one larger.

"Was that really first contact?" asked one of the smaller ones a bit disappointed.

"Of a sort, yes." replied the larger one. "But not the one that we deem as 'The' first contact. That comes later. This, however, is the first time that ordinary Smarians realised that their world wasn't the only one in existence. That there were other worlds with other living beings out there. The first time that they saw the creators of the machines that had landed before. Now they knew they weren't alone and that their world was being watched."

"Did they make the connection between themselves and the 'creatures' in the machines?" asked another.

"No. only a few knew that secret at this moment in time. The ordinary Smarian hadn't a clue of what these 'creatures' had come from or why. They still hadn't learnt the truth about their own origins yet, let alone the origins of these 'creatures'. And how they were connected. These were things for the future, not now. This landing was to mark the end of their age of innocence. An awakening to a new age and a new understanding of their world and what lies beyond it. The dawn of a time of great discoveries and the lifting of a veil of secrecy that had covered their world for a long, long time. Some will fight to keep the old ways and hide the past but a few will forge onwards and shine a light of hope on things that had been kept in the dark for a millennium. But that's another story and not for today! Now, it's back to the classroom and on with your lessons."

"Can't we stay a little longer and watch them celebrate? The way they dance makes me laugh!" asked another one of the smaller lights.

"No. Time travel might not mean much to us now but time wasting certainly does! Come on! We have work to do and much to learn." And with that the lights all disappeared.

The next day, they made their way back towards the base. Their job here was done. They had been out of radio contact with the base since coming out the other side of the mountain and Ha'an was beginning to wonder what he would report. Did he tell the truth about the machines and what they saw inside them? Did he mention Nerak? Did he just deny all of it and say that there was nothing there when they got there? This and many other questions were running through his head during the long march back towards the mountain.

A few days later, they had arrived at the foot of the mountain by the entrance to the caves. As they made camp that night, he looked around at his compatriots. Tega, the man who had spent many years alone on Topside and "Happy to be that way!" was now sitting down talking happily with Nerak and the others as if he always belonged there. Karel was still marvelling at the wide open spaces and the multitude of stars in the heavens. A new fascination for them after recent events! Krun, although being ignored by Karel, was lecturing on about positive thought and how to live life with no boundaries. Dez was rather disturbingly still talking to the scorse to which he had made such a connection with. The two were now inseparable and were the best of friends. Each putting up with the others' faults. The scorse, with its smelly nature and Dez and his complaining. Athan, the giant that once cowered in a corner and tried to hide himself away for fear of ridicule for being so big, now walked tall and with pride as he should. His confidence now as big as he was himself. Then there was Nerak. She who had walked into their lives and brightened up their world. Her stories of great civilisations that existed before Smar and her enthusiasm for life like a breath of fresh air. Something in short supply when you spend as much time as they had with a scorse in tow. He knew he couldn't mention her to base as they would just find her and return her to Below and she would never be allowed Topside again. She may even be thrown into the same asylum as her beloved professor Snikwah for talking such nonsense by the Great Council. No, he would protect her by keeping her out of any official report. He owed her that at least, he was still pondering on what to report, when Tega and Nerak came over and sat either side of him.

"Ha'an," Nerak started as you would expect. "Tega and I have something to tell you."

Ha'an looked first at Nerak, then Tega and back again at Nerak. After all, it was her that started speaking first and she was a lot easier on the eye than the old worn out face of Tega.

"Tega has agreed to let me stay and work with me on Topside. To continue searching in the mountain and some other places that he knows that may have some significant findings for my research."

Agreed to let her stay! thought Ha'an. *Like he had a choice in the matter. Like Nerak actually needed anyone's permission to do anything that she had already made up her mind to do! Nice though that she had convinced Tega that it was his decision.*

Nerak continued on, not noticing that Ha'an was having any thoughts at all.

"And Karel has asked to join us in our search."

"Seems the boy actually likes it out here!" added Tega somewhat confused. "So I said I would teach him all about being a scout and how to survive out here. I can pass on all the knowledge that Hundrey had passed on to me. Also I can tell Nerak about all the weird stories that Hundrey would tell me and show her the places that he said were once inhabited by our ancestors. Let her see if there was any evidence that what he said was true. I would like to think that not all that he said were just fireside tales."

There was a brief silence as both looked at Ha'an expecting some kind of response. Nothing happened for a while until Ha'an slowly broke into a grin. Then a smile and finally a laugh! Nerak and Tega sat back rather surprised at this reaction. They had thought that he would object and would protest but this was not the reaction that either of them had anticipated. They looked at each other somewhat confused and then back at Ha'an.

"And why not!" blurted out Ha'an at last. "Makes perfect sense to me. Karel has always got his head either looking up at the sky or just looking in awe at this inhospitable landscape as if it was a home form home anyway. He will make an excellent scout! Tega, you will have a student that will make you proud, I'm sure. And as for you, Nerak." Ha'an paused for a moment. He wanted to say just how much he had enjoyed her company over these past few weeks. That she had kept him sane in his darkest of moments. He knew that Nerak was a free spirit and her path was very different to most. Her path that would lead her on to many more great adventures and discoveries. He just felt grateful that their paths had crossed for a brief moment in time and that he had the opportunity to meet this extraordinary person. To travel at least part of the way with her on her journey through life. Who knows? Their paths may even cross again one day! Nerak looked at him as if she knew exactly what he was thinking. "And as for you, Nerak. I think that you have made the right decision. Go and prove to us all that we are not the first Smarians to have lived here. Go prove your professor Snikwah right and make us proud. Let me be able to shout out loud that I once knew the great doctor Nerak Catall! The bravest of all Smarians before she was famous!"

Nerak leapt forward and hugged him much to Ha'an's delight.

"Thank you!" she whispered into his ear and gave him a peck on the cheek.

"Well, that's sorted then!" said Tega who turned, smiled and gave a thumbs up to Karel.

"Yippee!" declared Karel and started to jump around. Krun was a bit taken aback. He had never had this reaction to one of his lectures on positive thought before! Most people just went away to contemplate about what he has said not jump around shouting "Yippee!" it was a while before he realised what the reason really was for Karel's jubilation but he still held onto the thought that it was his teachings of positive thought that had brought about Karel's good fortune.

The rest of the evening was spent discussing what would happen the next day and how they would report all that had happened. Karel was so pleased to be staying at Topside that he couldn't sleep. No more Below for him! He was going to be a scout on Topside for the rest of his life. Everyone was in a joyous mood and were dancing around the campfire yet again until the early hours.

The next day, they said their goodbyes and the two groups went their separate ways not knowing if they would ever meet again. As Ha'an entered the mouth of the cave through the mountain, he took one last look at Nerak, Tega and Karel. He waved them goodbye for the last time and headed into the mountain.

"Will we ever see them again?" asked Dez not to anyone in particular at all.

"Oh, I think so," said Ha'an. "Don't know where or when but I just have this feeling that we will see them again."

"Good!" replied Dez. "I liked them. They are my friends!"

Ha'an laughed.

"After all that we have been through together, we are all your friends. Now let's get through this mountain and back to base. I've a feeling that there are a lot of people going to be interested in what we have to say."

He wasn't wrong!

Chapter 14
Back to Below

Once they had reached the other side of the mountain and had emerged into the sunlight from the depths of these strangely formed caves, they radioed back to base that their return was imminent and that they had indeed a story to tell. To prepare for the amazing details of, not just one but the many different types of machines that they had encountered and what they had seen was in them. Of the enormous bubble machine that these huge machine beings roamed around Topside inside of. The sheer size of the massive main dome and the strange green plants that the machine beings tended to so carefully. Their purpose unknown. Perhaps to see if the plants from their own world could survive on Smar ready for future visits or invasion. Of the abduction of the scorse and their dramatic rescue of him and escape from one of these beings. Obviously leaving out the part played by Nerak to protect her presence on Topside as agreed. To tell them that there was a massive site for scientific research left by these beings from beyond their planet. Objects that would have to be studied in situ as they were far too big to be extradited to 'The' place. All the way back Ha'an, Athan, Krun and Dez ran through their story so as to make sure that all said the same thing and none let slip about Nerak.

As the base came into view their pace quickened. No longer the bunch of misfit volunteers that left the base in the middle of the night weeks ago. They had survived the trials and tribulations of Topside and the beings with their machines from beyond. Now they were all brothers. Brothers that had made it back when none expected them to. A friendship forged in the wastelands and mountains of Topside. As they approached the main gates the guards opened them, stood to attention and saluted our returning heroes.

Well I didn't expect that! thought Ha'an as he returned their salute. *That's definitely never happened before!*

He quickly looked to see if someone important was following in behind them but there was no one there. The salute really had been for them!

They walked in to see the usual sight of new recruits going through their marching routines whilst being shouted at by the officers in charge. Others were just running around the parade ground with their packs on again whilst being shouted at and chased by the officers. A familiar pattern that was basic training. No one dare give them a second glance for fear of the officers stick in the ribs. Some of the older recruits were wandering around with a clip board and looking at different things, nodding to each other and writing something down. Probably nothing at all but it looked good. No one asked questions of a Smarian with a clip board as it was assumed that they were always doing something important. Why else would they have been given a clip board! Nothing had changed. As they made their way towards the main office they could see the commandant followed by two officers making their way across the parade ground towards them. Ha'an and the guys out their kit down and stood to attention. Awkward salutes out the way the commandant started to congratulate them.

"Well done chaps! I knew if we sent our best men, you'd do it! The base has been bursting with the news of your success. Although, obviously no one is to know exactly what it is that you were successful at. Can't have that kind of news broadcasted to the civilian world now, can we?" waffled on the commandant.

Best men! thought Ha'an. *Not quite what was implied before we left! Expendables had been a more accurate term.*

The commandant continued on.

"You're all to go to Below on the next transport to be debriefed by the General himself and his staff. Get a good night's rest. Eat and drink as much as you like and relax. You must be exhausted! I think the coming are going to be somewhat busy for all of you. Erm, you seem to be one shy of your compliment that left? Did he survive the trip?"

It had taken the commandant this long to realise that they were one short.

"Yes sir. Private Karel, sir." replied Ha'an. "Took to Topside so well that he asked to be trained by our scout Tega. A brave soldier who wants to serve the Smarian people by staying Topside and reporting any events that threaten our safety, sir. A fearless recruit who would give his life to save others, sir."

Ha'an had visions of Karel running around with the rest of them, throwing things and screaming as the machine being chased them. His shrills of "Help!" and "Don't kill me!" still ringing in Ha'an's ears. But Karel still did it despite all his fears. He had still put himself in the line of danger to help the others and that meant a lot.

"Well, not often we get a volunteer for being a scout on Topside. Good for him!" replied a somewhat bemused commandant for most recruits wanted nothing more than to return to Below as soon as possible. Him included!

"Perhaps there was something wrong with the chap? Wanting to be Topside? Who on Smar would want that?" thought the commandant but didn't waste any more of his valuable time on the matter.

The commandant told them that there were a lot of people anxious to hear what they had to report about their epic encounter with the machine beings. Scientists and clerics alike all wanting to hear this incredible story. The scientists to ensure funds for their studies of the objects from the previous landings and more to examine the remains left behind by these beings from another world. The clerics to discredit it as nothing more than an over imaginative delusion brought on by Topside madness! The objects planted there by those wishing to deceive the Smarian people into thinking that there was more out there than the clerics would have them believe. To undermine the entire Smarian religion! The Great One himself was particularly interested in hearing their report. After all, He had been the one to send them there in the first place and liked a good yarn!

Athan didn't hear much of what the commandant had said.

"Eat and drink as much as you like!" had stuck in his head. Rations had never been enough for Athan and he was going to make the most of the "as much as you like" as he could.

Krun was busy seeing the bright side of their return as he too liked the idea of the "as much as you like!"

"See! Every outcome has a positive if you look hard enough for it!" he had thought as he and Athan headed straight for the canteen once they were dismissed closely followed by Ha'an.

Dez made his way to the barn where the scorse were kept. He found a nice spot for Woc and himself and there he stayed. He wasn't going to be separated from his friend. Athan and Krun had said that they would bring him plenty of food to eat once they had their fill. Something that might take a while in Athan's case but Dez was prepared to wait for his friends to return. One of the other recruits, seeing what Dez was doing, had started to say something rather condescending to Dez about his closeness to the scorse. However, seeing that Athan had turned around and was now standing behind Dez clenching his plate sized fists ready to defend his little friend, had decided against finishing it. A very wise move really. In fact no one was going to attempt to bully or say a bad word about Dez and his Woc ever again for the same reason.

The following day they were transported back to Below and straight to the grandeur of the generals office. Woc had been left outside tied to a post with a big bag of food. He was quite content to stay there to happily eat and fart away. The knot tying him to the post checked by Ha'an as still no one trusted Dez's rope skills. Now the commandant had found it strange that they had all on taking this scorse with them. Normally the scorse were just assigned to another party about to leave the confines of the base but he had gone along with it anyway. They were the heroes of the day so why not! Plus the fact that Dez had been given the honour of 'Keeper of the scorse' at Ha'an's request. A request that the commandant thought more of a punishment rather than a reward. Dez, on the other hand, thought this a great opportunity. Now he wouldn't have to be separated from Woc nor do the other things associated with basic training. Exercise and marching! It would also hold him in good stead for the job that Krun had offered him working with the scorse on his parents' ranch. Result!

"Welcome!" said the General as the four were escorted into his office by his secretary closely followed by the Herald. The contempt between Mildread and the Herald still very apparent as they smiled coldly at each other as each tried to keep up the faint illusion of politeness.

"Please take a seat and tell me all about your adventure. I have seen Sergeant Ha'an's report, of course, but thought best hear it directly from the scorse's mouth!" he continued as they sat. The Herald stood at the back of the office. He already knew the secret of the visitors chairs and so offered them to the others smiling. Athan also stood as, after one aborted attempt, he realised that there was no way that he would fit in that chair!

The general listened intently with the occasional "I see" and "Aha" as they related the events that had befallen them on their mission to Topside. Of the storm, the mountain and finally their encounter with these beings from somewhere other than Smar. In fact the General had at points seemed quite interested. However, there had also been points where the General had nearly nodded off. The occasional and loud diplomatic cough from the Herald being the only thing keeping him awake. The Herald being somewhat experienced as to having to keep the General awake during such meetings. Listening to others go on and on about something that had happened to them wasn't something that he was any good at.

Having others listen to him as he talked about himself… well that was always a pleasure! After what seemed to the General to be about an hour he announced that they were all to have lunch in the Great Chambers restaurant. This was normally reserved for the Great Council members only but had been sanctioned by the Great One himself. A great honour plus the fact that it was free! It hadn't even been probably more than fifteen minutes either but as the General had skipped elevenses he was more concerned about his stomach than a report that someone else was going to read anyway. The information was for the scientists and the clerics to mull over and decipher not him. All he was interested in was the final report and the recommendations of what to do. That and what was on the menu for today!

After a humongous lunch, with the general and Athan competing as to who could eat and drink the most and a stern warning to them about not talking to anyone about their adventures Topside, the General sent them all on leave for three whole weeks. They could go wherever they wanted, do whatever they wanted and all at the expense of the Smarian people. A fitting reward for what they had endured. Three weeks on the beaches of the Medaciffic Sea they had all decided. Five-star luxury. Good food good drinks and good friends. What more could they ask for? Oh, and yes, Dez could even take his scorse with him!

A strange request, thought the General. *Most people want money or something more along those lines rather than taking a scorse on holiday! Each to their own I suppose.* And thought no more about it.

After they had gone, the General meandered his way to the Great Chamber to see the Great One who was having tea with the information minister. Athan had been a formidable opponent in the eating and drinking stakes and the General was feeling slightly worse for wear because of it. Never one to turn down such a challenge the General felt sure that he had succeeded in winning the contest as he waddled his way rather unsteadily down the corridor. The guards, too, had noticed that the Generals half-hearted attempt at a salute whilst having a silly smile on his face and giggling to himself was worse than usual. They just smiled at each other as he passed through into the Great Chamber. The General, pulling himself together as best he could, continued his way along the familiar red carpet to where the Great One and the Information minister were happily gorging on tea and cakes.

"Ah General. Please come and join us." the Great One said as He beckoned the General to sit at the table. Not wishing to appear rude, the General sat next to the Great One and helped himself to a large cup of tea and the largest cake he could find on the plate.

"Did our heroes have much more to tell us?" asked the Great One in between feeding His face with one of the many cream cakes available.

"Not really." replied the General already halfway through his cake.

"Although I suspect that they aren't telling us everything." He continued as He made a grab for his second cake.

"There were parts that seemed somewhat vague to say the least. Like there was someone else out there that they didn't want to tell us about. Someone who was a big part of the operation but who shouldn't have been out there at all! Obviously I'll have to wait for the full report to confirm this."

"Probably the minister of Foreign Affair's daughter." the Information minister said in a very casual way.

"We know she's out there somewhere looking for lost civilisations. Lost track of her once she jumped off one of the transports going to the base on Topside. Hooked up with one of the scouts probably. Intelligent girl. It's a shame we can't tell her the truth and save her the bother. If only we could trust her not to say anything but we can't. Made that mistake with her professor Snikwah and look where he ended up. All he had to do was join the team and keep quiet about his work but no. No, he had to go and try and tell the whole of Smar as if they had the right to know. They couldn't cope with the truth. Not yet anyway."

"Which reminds me," interrupted the Great One as He lent forward for His third cake. "Are we going to have any more trouble form that snoopy journalist? Hmm?"

"None at all." replied the Information minister. A wry smile covering his face.

"Why she is at this moment investigating a very special story on Topside for us. A story that only someone with the correct journalistic skills and experience such as she has could possibly uncover. A story of our ancestors and the old world. Of what they did and where they went. Mind you, only if she survives out there long enough to tell the tale of course! Ha ha!"

And they all began to laugh. Laugh and eat and drink. Just another day in politics!

Somewhere out on Topside, a very frustrated angry Smarian journalist was shouting obscenities whilst watching as the transport left her in the middle of nowhere. Mr Tash was smiling and waving from the back as it moved off into the distance.

"Let us know if you find anything, won't you?" he shouted. "Don't be a stranger, will you!" and with that he sat back in a corner of the transport and laughed.

Asil was furious that she had fallen for such a cheap trick. To be dumped out on topside and told that the proof for her story was all around her.

"Everything that you read is true. About the landings, the ancestors living on Topside and the existence of 'The' place! All the proof she would ever need to vindicate herself was there on Topside to be found. All she had to do was find it!" they had said.

How could she have been so naive! She walked back into the cave where they had put her rations, maps and meagre belongings paying no attention to the very clear symbols above the strangely square entrance. The ancient symbols that they had spoken of that could help her. Unaware that the truth really was out there for her to find if only she would look with an open mind. If only she would look up at the ancient words that spelt out 'The Smarian National Library!'

The End?

Or just the beginning!